Conquest
Lara Rios

Wise Writer Pubishing

Conquest

Published by WISE WRITER PUBLISHING

Amante, Julia, 1967-

Conquest / Julia Amante - Second Edition 2025

ISBN: 978-1-931627-15-3

    1. Enemies to Lovers Romance – Fiction

    2. Contemporary Romance – Fiction

    3. Christmas – Fiction

    4. Latino Romance

Book Cover by The Killion Group Inc.

Praise for Lara Rios's Novels

Conquest

Her characters come to life right before your eyes from the very first word.

> —Robin Peek - Under the Covers

Lara Rios pens an enjoyable romance with a unique premise in Conquest.

> —Rickey R. Mallory - Painted Rock Reviews

Ms. Rios humanizes Tess and Logan by showing their family relationships and the forces that made them the people they are. She shows their strengths and vulnerabilities, their tenderness and passion, and intersperses the serious with the humourous.

—Jane Bowers - Romance Reviews Today

Ms. Rios succeeds in bringing out the best in both characters and leaving the reader wanting more.

—Addicted2Romancebooks.com

Lara Rios has a nice breezy style to her writing and keeps you interested in her charming characters.

—Suzanne Coleburn - The Belles and Beaux of Romance

"A big, beautiful novel of love, family, and the close-knit community they inhabit. By turns touching, funny, tragic, and triumphant, it's the story of an endearing group of people in search of their own American dream."

—Susan Wiggs, New York Times bestselling author

"Julia Amante understands the ties that bind all families regardless of culture and nationality—the struggle

for identity, the importance of dream, and above all, love. I truly enjoyed Evenings at the Argentine Club."

—Jill Marie Landis, New York Times bestselling author

Built to Win

Lara Rios delivers a dynamite story rich with emotion, deeply passionate characters, and breath-taking sensuality!

—Best Selling Temptation author, Janelle Denison

Unforgettable characters in a compelling story about the enduring spirit of the heart.

—Meryl Sawyer - author of TRUST NO ONE

Contents

1. Dear Reader   1

2. CHAPTER ONE   3

3. CHAPTER TWO   9

4. CHAPTER THREE   17

5. CHAPTER FOUR   25

6. CHAPTER FIVE   31

7. CHAPTER SIX   42

8. CHAPTER SEVEN   49

9. CHAPTER EIGHT   55

10. CHAPTER NINE   64

11. CHAPTER TEN   74

12. CHAPTER ELEVEN   80

13. CHAPTER TWELVE   90

14. CHAPTER THIRTEEN   101

15. CHAPTER FOURTEEN   111

16. CHAPTER FIFTEEN   119

17. CHAPTER SIXTEEN   130

18. CHAPTER SEVENTEEN   138

19. CHAPTER EIGHTEEN   151

20. CHAPTER NINETEEN   158

21. CHAPTER TWENTY   167

22. CHAPTER TWENTY-ONE   176

23. TEN YEARS LATER   187

Here is a special advanced preview of: 198

24. Built to Win   199

25. CHAPTER ONE   200

Dedication   215

Acknowledgements   216

About the author   217

Dear Reader

I'm so excited for the re-release of Conquest! Every book has its story, so I'd like to briefly share how Conquest was born:

I had dreamed of being a writer since I was a teen, so when an editor called to reject my manuscript for a novel I'd spent over a year writing, I was devastated. *Why was she calling to reject me?*

"But I think you have talent," she said. "Do you have another story idea?"

I had many ideas, but nothing was written. The stories were all in my head.

"Yeah," I said. "I'm writing a shipboard romance." That thought came to me, not because I was writing anything, but because my husband and I were leaving the next week on a cruise that circled South America. It left Chile and rounded Cape Horn, stopping at various Argentine ports, ending in Buenos Aires.

The movie *Titanic* was one of the most popular movies that year, so my claim to be writing a romance that took place on a cruise ship had appeal to my editor. "Perfect," she said. "Send me a partial."

A partial consists of sample chapters and a synopsis.

So, I went on my cruise and took a massive notebook with me, determined to have the book finished by the end of the cruise. I wrote on the decks of the ship, in my cabin, while enjoying high tea, late at night, early in the morning; I handwrote the entire first draft of the book that eventually became *Conquest*.

Conquest was my first published book, and it launched my writing career. I sold three additional romances to that publisher, then two more to another publisher. My dream of becoming a writer had become a reality, and it all started with this little enemies-to-lovers novel. Eventually, I switched to writing women's fiction under the pseudonym Julia Amante, publishing six additional novels.

But we never forget our first.

Now, twenty-five years later, I am re-releasing *Conquest*. I tried to keep the original flavor of the novel. I kept what I consider today imperfections of a beginning writer. But I edited anything dated. For example, in one scene, she waits for an answering machine to pick up a call. No one has an answering machine anymore since we carry our cell phones with us, and unanswered calls go to voicemail. She also had a newspaper delivered, which tends to be rare these days. So, I modernized the story while keeping most of it identical to the original.

I also added a final chapter, following the couple ten years later. I always thought the original novel ended too abruptly, but I had to adhere to page count limits back then.

I hope you will enjoy re-reading *Conquest*, or reading it for the first time if you didn't know me back in 2000 when the book was released. And I hope you enjoy the luxurious journey that takes Teresa and Logan to the starkly beautiful Patagonia at the end of the world, where the characters find beauty and love.

CHAPTER ONE

Teresa Romero dropped her purse on her desk and slumped down on her rolling leather chair, which screeched as she leaned back. She took a deep, steadying breath. She was never late for work, but today the gods just weren't on her side.

Not only had she had an ant invasion in her kitchen to contend with when she woke up, and a wet mail to spread out on the living room table because her neighbor refused to fix his sprinkler that hit her mailbox, but on her way to work, the fan belt on her old Toyota Celica finally gave out. She had to walk three blocks in high heels to the Mobile station and persuade the greasy, overworked mechanic to fix her car ahead of the other jobs he had waiting in line. An hour and a half later, she was on her way to Los Angeles again, determined to reach the black and white building which housed the offices of Penguin Apparel Inc.

"Hey Tess," Krystle, a busybody sales rep, paused by her desk. "Heard you got the big Patagonia account."

Teresa frowned. "Where'd you hear that?"

Krystle shrugged. "It's going around." Krystle was physically the blond equivalent of Teresa: large breasts, wide hips, too thin for the large body frame. Qualities that made Teresa self-conscious because of the male attention they attracted. In fact, she tried to minimize the exaggerated shapeliness of her body with respectable business suits. In contrast, Krystal chose clothes that were too tight, too revealing. Teresa admired Krystal for her courage in proudly showing her body, yet she cringed at the spectacle she made of herself.

"Well," Teresa said, placing her purse in the bottom drawer of her desk and straightening in her chair. "No decision's been made, as far as I know."

Her line rang, giving Teresa an excuse to brush Krystle off and get to work. She lifted the receiver to her ear and wiggled her fingers at Krystle; however, she didn't take the hint. She stood in front of Teresa's desk, smiling and listening. From the one-sided conversation, she would, no doubt, decipher what she could and embellish the rest.

Edward Reed's voice eclipsed Teresa's thoughts about Krystle. Mr. Reed wanted to see her in his office right away. *Great, I'm late one day, and the boss notices.* She let him know she was on her way.

"Did he say you got the account?" Krystle asked, eager to spread the gossip. Everyone in the office knew she and Logan Wilde were competing for this account, and she was sure they'd probably even started a pool betting on the one they thought would win.

"No, sorry, Krystle. He didn't say what he wanted."

Teresa left a disillusioned Krystle behind and headed to Edward Reed's office. He welcomed her with a smile. Maybe he wasn't going to lecture her about getting to work on time. Could it be that she actually did get the Patagonia account? Penguin was launching its new wool apparel next season, and all they needed was to set up a reliable supplier for wool. *El Gaucho Estancia* in Argentina was that supplier, and Teresa knew she could handle the buy.

"How are you today, Tess?" he asked absently, barely looking up from a file on his desk.

"Not bad," she lied. Her feet were killing her from walking those three blocks in cute, but uncomfortable Michael Kors pumps. She also noticed a grease smudge on her pale blue skirt that no one else would see. "Is something wrong?"

"No, actually, I think you're going to be pleased with my news."

Though she wasn't asked to, Teresa took a seat, her excitement level going up a few notches. "The Patagonia account?"

"As a matter of fact—"

"Sorry I'm late." Logan Wilde blew in, took a seat beside Teresa, and with the theatrics that typified Logan, gave an exaggerated angelical smile. She was sure *that* was the smile he used to vie for everyone's adoration in the office. He had women jumping to help him take care of his mail, clean his desk, type his reports, and listen to his sob stories about his kids.

"It's all right, it seems you're both running late today," Reed commented.

Logan turned a shocked expression toward Teresa. "*You* were late?"

She ignored the urge to fire back that, unlike his everyday tardiness, this was her first time in three years. She lifted her chin " You were saying, Edward?"

Logan eased his long, wiry body back, overly relaxed, overly confident. "The moment of truth, huh boss?"

"I was just telling Tess that she will be pleased with my decision."

Logan's bright smile dimmed just a touch, and that satisfied her almost as much as what Reed was saying.

"Go on," Logan said.

Edward Reed cleared his throat. "I've thought long and hard about this, and I've found reasons why each of you deserves this account."

Teresa held her breath.

"Tess, you're excellent with people, you put in long hours . . . ." Reed looked at Logan. "And you're a great closer, Logan, a great negotiator."

Teresa and Logan glanced at each other. This was an exciting account, the opportunity to travel to a remote farm at the end of the world. More importantly, it came with a commission that would allow her to pay off her parents' debts and guarantee they didn't lose their family restaurant.

"I've decided," Reed said with a smile. "That I'm going to send you both."

The room was silent. Had she heard right?

"You want to run that by me again?" Logan was actually frowning. She'd never seen a frown on that overly happy, childish face.

"I believe together you can secure the buy and get us the wool account we need. One of you might be able to pull it off, but with you both, we can't lose. Now let's go over the figures——"

"Whoa, wait a minute." Logan stood. "I don't need her tagging along. I can close the deal on my own."

"Well, I certainly don't need you." Teresa's face warmed. *The nerve of that man!*

"No offense, sweetheart, but—"

"My name is Teresa."

"Whatever. He's just letting you go because you're Mexican."

"What?" She bolted out of her seat. "I can't believe you just said that."

"Oh, come on, Tess, I didn't mean that as a racial jab, and you know it. He wants you to translate. I don't need a translator."

"Logan," Reed said harshly. "Sit down, you're being offensive."

"I've never needed help to close an account before."

Neither have I, she felt like screaming back at him, but arguing was senseless. She took her seat.

Reed sighed. "If you must know, Logan, Tess was my first choice. Her language skills are definitely a plus, but besides that, she's a great buyer. I think in this case, though, you're going into macho territory with those sheep shearers, and they're going to want to see male representation. I've thought this through. You're both going."

Logan glared at Teresa. Did he think *she* was pleased with this? Spending the next few weeks with God's gift to women was hardly her idea of fun. Of all the men in her office, she had to get stuck with this arrogant, self-centered jerk. But even worse than that, she'd have to split the commission with him, money she could have given her parents.

He slumped into his chair again. "What am I supposed to be, her bodyguard?"

"You'll have to figure out how you want to approach this. One of you does the talking, the other the paperwork and planning? You decide on the best strategy. The key is to secure the buy at the lowest possible cost. Understand?"

They both nodded.

"Good. When you get there, I want you to tour the Estancia, check out the operation, do quality tests, and if all looks good, arrange the buy."

They both listened silently. Teresa felt she was being handed down a sentence.

"You'll have plenty of time to plan." Edward Reed grinned, and he opened up a file. Leaning forward, he handed a brochure to each of them. "This is the good news. You'll be on a cruise ship which will dock close to the sheep Estancia. It will take you about a week to get there since there are no airports where you're going."

No airports? "But there *is* a small airport in the Santa Cruz province, I read about it when I did my research," Teresa said.

"Well," Reed said. "Technically, you're right, but it's used mostly for cargo. Passenger crafts come in about once a week, and not during the holidays."

"So we're going on a cruise ship?" She asked, unbelieving.

"You sure are," Reed said, the pitch of his voice and enthusiastic gestures indicating he thought he'd just granted her the greatest gift. "Of course, I'm not being too generous. Like I said, since it's the holidays, most transportation won't be running in Argentina. A ship is about the only way to get you there comfortably."

"Can't we drive from Buenos Aires?" Logan asked.

"Believe me, you don't want to drive. Most of the roads in Patagonia, if you can call them that, aren't even paved. No, you'll fly into Buenos Aires and from there, take the ship down the coast."

Teresa's brain was still registering something else he said. "You want us to leave before Christmas?"

"That's right. It's a Christmas/New Year's cruise which will get you to San Julian at the beginning of January. Sheep shearing's done in the summer—their summer."

Teresa's spirit dropped a few more notches. She glanced at Logan, but besides having to share the account with her, he seemed to have no objections. He sat quietly listening, almost brooding.

"I see." Teresa's voice couldn't conceal her disappointment. She'd never missed Christmas with her close family. This would be the first time.

"So, put your other accounts on hold. You leave in a week."

CHAPTER TWO

T eresa took her sealed envelopes to the mail drop that evening. As she was walking back to her desk, she saw a shadow standing beside the file cabinets at the entrance to the room. Everyone else was long gone, or they should have been.

"Who's there?" She hurried behind her desk, where she could pull out sharp scissors if needed.

"Just me, Tess," Logan stepped forward, dressed casually in faded jeans and a denim button-up shirt. He was bathed in soft moonlight, bringing out reddish highlights in his normal coffee colored hair.

Teresa sat, relieved. Logan was annoying, but at least he wasn't dangerous.

He took a seat in front of her desk and folded his long arms on her stacks of papers. He leaned his chin on his arms in such an adorable boyish pose that Teresa had to look away or risk losing some of that well built-up anger.

"Still upset, huh?"

"I'm just finishing my work, Logan. What are you doing here? You couldn't possibly have come back to get any work done."

"No? And why couldn't I possibly be here to work?"

"Because you don't work, you play. You don't take anything seriously. You treat all your accounts as if they were just a game." She ignored his intense gaze.

"Think so?"

She flashed him the best 'oh please' look she could manage.

He smiled, only the corners of his lips lifting a bit, as if he were too tired to do any better. Then he sat back. "There's enough to be serious about without adding work to that list."

Teresa bounced her pen on her desk, and it clicked as the point appeared and disappeared. "I take my work very seriously."

"I've noticed."

"I could have handled the wool buy without you." She wanted it to be clear that she didn't need him along on what should have been her account.

"I could have handled it without you as well. In fact, I like to work alone."

"It should have been mine. I worked hard for it."

He chuckled. "That's a good reason."

She stopped clicking the pen and flung it on her paperwork, crossing her arms across her chest. "And what's your reason? You're Reed's good friend?"

"Give it up, Tess." His voice hardened. "I've got twice the experience. I'm a better closer, admit it."

"You are not."

"I close ninety-five percent of my accounts. What's your percentage?"

"I don't know, I never—"

"It's eighty-five percent, very good I admit, but . . . I can drive a harder bargain. You're good at putting the deal down on paper. So that's the way I think we should handle this account. Let me do the talking."

This time Teresa laughed contemptuously. "I thought I was going to do the talking. I'm the Mexican, remember?"

He sighed. "I didn't mean to sound so rude today. I was just as surprised by Edward's decision as you were. I either win or lose, there's no in between."

"Is that supposed to be an apology?"

"Just don't add bigot to my long list of defects, okay?"

She gave him a half-shrug, half-nod. Logan may be a lot of things, but a racist, he wasn't. He liked everyone, regardless of race or age. Everyone, it seemed, but her.

Logan stood and came around her desk. He rested his jean-sculpted bottom on her desk top and leaned forward. "Listen, Teresa, neither of us likes the fact that we have to share this account, but we *can* do this together. What do you say?"

This was the closest she'd ever been to Logan. Although they worked in the same office, she avoided him as much as possible. Even during staff meetings, she learned not to meet his eyes since he always seemed to have a mocking glint in them. Tonight, he didn't.

She noticed for the first time what beautiful hazel eyes he had, large orbs which seemed to soak in whatever he was looking at, and long, thick eyelashes which curved at the ends. His neck was strong with an exaggerated, protruding Adam's apple as if he were still a teenager growing into his body parts. He wasn't handsome—she didn't think so anyway—but those eyes, she could definitely stare into them all night. She shook herself mentally. What was she thinking?

"We'll work together, Logan, as long as you don't try to tell me how to do my job," she answered, ignoring the scent of baby shampoo that clung to his body. Baby shampoo? He must have been with the kids. It was hard to be upset with a man who smelled like an infant.

He winked. "You'll thank me when this is over. You'll learn a thing or two about how negotiating really works." He straightened and moved away. "Night, Tess."

And just like that, she was angry all over again.

***

"Oh, stop moping. I wish someone would give me an all-expense-paid cruise as part of my job." Karen tapped Logan's knee.

Logan sank low in his chair at his sister's kitchen table, knees wide apart and head hung between his shoulders. Tomorrow he'd be on a plane to Buenos Aires. He'd come to say goodbye to Karen and his four-year-old nephew and seven-year-old niece and to bring them their Christmas presents. "Yeah, that part sounds all right. I don't like leaving you and the kids alone for the holidays though, Karen."

Since Andy and Stacy's so-called father rarely showed up for the holidays, Logan always liked to be there. Of course, he could have admitted defeat by letting Tess go to Argentina alone and take the account, but his pride wouldn't allow it. He didn't need to look into Teresa's smug face and let her think she got one over on him.

"We'll be fine. I'm taking them to Disneyland. They can hardly wait."

Logan smiled. "I bet." He lifted his bottom off the chair and reached into his back pocket, pulling out his wallet. "Here." He handed her a few bills across the table.

"No, Logan. I'm not taking your money." She picked up the coffee cups and walked them to the sink.

"You are. Buy the kids whatever they want at Disney. If I can't be there, at least I want them to have mementos to show me when I get back."

She came back to the table and fingered the bills. "Logan, this is too much."

He frowned at her. "Nothing is too much for them. You and the kids are the only family I have."

She gave him a loving, thankful smile. Whatever she was about to say was lost as Andy came running into the room, jumped on Logan's lap, and faced Karen.

"But why can't we open the presents now, Mom?" Andy whined.

"Because it's not Christmas yet." Karen returned to the sink and began washing the cups.

"Let them open one, Karen," Logan coaxed.

"Not until Christmas."

"But Uncle Lo-in won't be here. Pleeez."

Logan's heart did a flip. He should be here for Christmas. He growled and pretended to bite the little boy behind the neck. Andy squirmed and giggled and begged Logan to stop. Logan kissed the boy's head and put him down.

"Just one present tonight and the rest on Christmas. What do you say?"

"Okay!" Andy shouted.

Karen didn't look pleased. She had one hand on her hip, tightly gripping a dish towel.

"Just one." Logan gave his sister a begging look, much like Andy's.

"Logan, you're worse than the kids. When you're here, they break all the rules."

She had far too many rules. When she had the kids, she was way too young, and to compensate for her lack of parenting skills, she was overly strict. He picked Andy up and placed him on his shoulder. "Loosen up, little sis, it's Christmas."

Logan ran to the living room with Andy on his shoulder, hollering and laughing. Logan called Stacy and let each child open one of their gifts. Karen sat on the arm of the sofa, watching with an amused look on her face.

Logan sat beside his sister and smiled. "See, it didn't hurt."

She rumpled his hair and kissed the top of his head. "We're so lucky to have you."

He watched the kids who were on their knees, tearing into their presents, and sending colorful red and green paper flying above their heads. They shrieked with delight. Logan felt like the lucky one to be able to share in the raising of his nephew and niece. He loved making them happy. After a hug and kiss, they were off and playing.

"I guess I'd better go, Karen."

She draped an arm around his shoulder. "Have a good time and don't work too hard."

***

On Laurel Canyon Boulevard, he swerved into the left lane to get on the freeway. The sound of a piercing horn zooming past him warned that the lane was not free.

"Damn." His mind had been on Karen and the kids, and he hadn't been paying attention to what he was doing.

He clicked his turn signal this time, shot a glance over his left shoulder, and safely swerved over. The on-ramp circled and led him to the crowded freeway. He sighed. Now what? It was early, so going home alone sounded depressing. He'd already packed his bags for his trip. There wasn't anything else to do except sleep.

He rolled down his window. A cold breeze flapped his T-shirt sleeve. He flipped the radio on and hit the scan button. The first couple of stations he allowed to skip over, then he stopped at the third, Aerosmith's "I Don't Want to Miss a Thing", an oldie but a goodie. He tapped his fingers on the steering wheel and drove. He liked driving at night when the stream of headlights relaxed him.

The thought of spending the next few weeks with that uptight, driven Tess sure didn't excite him. Why couldn't Edward have assigned Mary Ann or Brenda? At least with them, he could look forward to having some fun. Teresa had a bug up her butt that prevented her from so much as smiling, much less having a good time. She probably wouldn't know how to have a good time if she were standing in the middle of Time Square on New Year's Eve. She was all business, so serious he wondered what she was trying to prove. Too bad because she was kind of cute—hell, she was a knockout. Generously built with all the right curves in all the right places. A man could take his time feeling his way up and down and over a curvaceous body like that.

Logan shook off the thought. What was he, crazy, entertaining thoughts like that about Tiger Tess? The idea of any man touching her was almost laughable.

Keeping one hand firmly on the steering wheel, he leaned across the passenger seat to pull out his flight ticket from the glove compartment and check the time of their departure.

Logan frowned. He had two sets of tickets, both his and Teresa's. Did she realize Logan had both? He glanced from traffic to the address on her ticket. He was close; he'd drop it off. In fact, they could decide on a time for him to pick her up in the morning. There was no point in leaving both their cars at LAX for so long. Maybe he'd get some brownie points for being so considerate.

CHAPTER THREE

T eresa hurried to her front door to see who was leaning on her doorbell. She flung the door open, and her stomach did a flip. There, on her doorstep, looking marvelous as always, was a smiling Logan Wilde. She self-consciously looked down at her cut-off jeans and waist-high T-shirt. She had no shoes, and her unruly hair hung loose.

"Logan," she found her voice. "Hi."

"Sorry to drop by unannounced, but I realized I have your plane tickets."

"My plane tickets?" She was going to log onto the website tonight and download them to her phone. She searched her brain for all she'd packed in her office on Friday. Surely, she had the flight information somewhere.

"Are you going to invite me in?"

Teresa raked some hair away from her face and took a step back, giving him an apologetic nod. "Sure."

He strolled in and looked around her living room. It annoyed her that he so casually barged into her home uninvited and examined her personal space. She squeezed her toes into the plush burgundy carpet, remembering that she looked like a slob. "Where are those tickets?"

He pulled them out of his back pocket with his right hand and fanned them a bit, then slapped them on his left hand. "Right here."

She extended her hand.

"You want me to toss them?"

No, she wanted him to come back to the front door, give her the tickets, and leave. Teresa closed the door and moved closer to him since he wasn't budging. He smiled when she took the envelope from him.

"Thank you for stopping by. I guess I'll see you tomorrow."

He nodded. "Bright and early. I'll pick you up at, what, five thirty?"

"Pick me up?" She sounded like such an idiot tonight, but he was the last person she'd ever expected to see in her home, so she was off balance. "I've got a ride."

"Oh, I thought we'd drive in together."

"No offense, Logan, but we'll be spending enough time together in the next few weeks. Let's not add any more time."

He shrugged as if he couldn't care less whether she went or not. "From you, no offense taken."

She offered him a tight smile. "All right then . . . ." She motioned toward the front door. He crossed his arms and lazily gazed up and down her barely clothed body. Those big brown eyes were looking at her in warm appreciation, which momentarily left her feeling vulnerable and unsure. He'd never looked at her like that before, and it brought a spreading heat to her body that started at her face and moved down her neck and chest.

"I've got company," she blurted out. "I don't mean to throw you out but—"

"Come on Teresa, what's holding you up—oh!" Her sister, Carla, came out of the kitchen as if on cue.

"Carla, a colleague of mine dropped by unexpectedly."

Carla stood beside Teresa and shot Logan a friendly smile. She elbowed Teresa in the ribs. "Introduce me."

Teresa sighed. "Logan, Carla. Carla, Logan. He was just leaving," she said in a rush.

"Well, that's too bad you have to dash off. I just finished making dinner, and you're welcome to stay."

No, he's not! Teresa wanted to shout.

Logan gave Teresa a satisfied smile. "Sure, I'd love to stay. I'm hungry."

"Are you sure you made enough, Carla, when Roberto and your kids show up . . . ?"

Carla waved Teresa's protests away before she could finish getting it all out. "You know I always make more than enough. Come into the kitchen Logan, and take a seat."

Logan followed Carla, and for the life of her, Teresa couldn't figure out why he was doing this. Probably a strategy to find out her weaknesses and then use them against her later. They might be sharing the account, but she was sure Logan intended to take most of the credit in the end.

Teresa trudged behind them, swearing silently to strangle Carla later. Logan sat at the oval kitchen table, where Carla brought him chips and salsa and a beer. The smell of Carla's fried corn tortillas permeated the kitchen.

"Sit down, Teresita, and chat with your guest. I'll finish up."

Teresa cast Carla a menacing look. "He's not my guest, he's yours. I'll set the table."

"Hmm," Logan scooped a mound of chunky salsa into his mouth. He shook his head with a look of ecstasy on his face. "This is great salsa."

"Glad you like it," Carla answered in her usual cheery manner.

"Did you make it?" He crossed an ankle over his opposite knee.

Teresa placed the plates, forks, glasses, and napkins on the table, ignoring him as much as possible. She thought she caught him looking at her bare legs, but she was probably just being paranoid.

"It's from my mother's restaurant," Carla called from the stove, over the sound of bubbling oil, where she continued frying more tortilla shells.

"Really?" He was being disgustingly charming as always, his flirtatious eyes expressing genuine interest. "She owns a restaurant?"

"*El Horno*, in Santa Monica," Carla volunteered.

Teresa didn't want to discuss her parents or their difficulties with the restaurant. "Another beer, Logan?"

He smiled. "No, thanks."

"The only one who can make salsa even half as good as mom is Teresa," Carla continued to feed him personal information.

"Really? I guess you're good at everything, aren't you?"

She sat beside him, trying to hide her half-dressed body behind the kitchen table. The heat from the stove sure was making the kitchen warm. Why was he staring at her with those intense brown eyes? Oh yeah, he asked her something. "I'm not that good a cook, trust me."

"Which is why she doesn't eat. She can't cook, so she doesn't eat." Carla was babbling. "She just keeps getting skinnier."

Teresa rolled her eyes. Carla sounded more like their mother every day.

Logan's eyes dropped below her shoulders, then he picked up a chip and loaded it with salsa. He leaned sideways, his shoulder touching hers. He brought the chip to her lips. "Open up."

If she opened her mouth to argue, he'd shove that salsa pack chip in her mouth, so she tilted her head back and shook her head.

"Come on, Tess, eat."

She was not about to let him feed her. Just the thought of his long, tapered fingers so close to her lips was excruciatingly unnerving.

She reached up and pinched the chip with her fingertips to take it from his hand. Their fingers touched, and immediately their eyes clashed. He let go of the chip and grazed the top of her index finger as he retreated. Her hand trembled.

Teresa was no longer hungry. Her stomach heaved, but she ate the chip. Since doing otherwise would be like admitting to Logan how nervous he was making her.

He gave her a mischievous grin, and she felt foolish.

Just as she was swallowing the spicy salsa, her brother-in-law, Roberto and the kids trumpeted through the front door. Carla's kids never did anything quietly. Logan jumped, twisting his head to look over his shoulder. The three kids came bouncing in, calling for Carla, all talking at once. Carla made them all wash their hands and sit at the table. Roberto kissed Carla, then Teresa, and sat beside Logan.

"Hey," he said to Logan.

Logan stuck out his hand. "Hey, man."

They shook.

"This your new dude, Tere?" Roberto loved to tease her. She cringed. *No, not with Logan, please.* "He's a co-worker, behave yourself."

Roberto and Logan began to talk about sports and cars. Carla brought the shredded beef tacos to the table, and they ate. Logan raved over her tacos, not to mention her mother's chips and salsa. Roberto and Logan finished off the bowl of chips. Just like at work, everyone loved Logan. What was wrong with people? Couldn't they see through him? He was so transparent to her.

Roberto rounded up the kids after they ate and took them to the living room, where they could play video games and scream without bothering the adults.

"Mexican food is my favorite. Thanks, Carla." Logan wiped his lips and patted his flat stomach.

"My pleasure, just take care of my little sister on this trip. We want her back safe and sound."

Teresa stood and gave Logan an apologetic smile. "I'm twenty-eight and I'm still her little sister."

Logan smiled and rested his arm on the back of the now empty chair beside him, looking so at home in her house. "I feel the same way about my younger sister. Are you the youngest, Tess?"

"Oh, how cute. Is that what he calls you?"

Teresa frowned at her sister. "That's what they all call me at work. She turned back to Logan. "I have two younger brothers, sixteen and fourteen.

Logan eyebrows went up. "Big family."

"Average."

"Not in my book."

Carla cleaned up and insisted that Teresa go finish her packing.

"I'm surprised she isn't packed yet," Logan commented as he brought their drinking glasses to the sink.

"Oh she is, but she has to recheck at least a half a dozen times or she feels she isn't ready. My sister is a bit neurotic; in case you haven't noticed."

Logan smiled. Why couldn't Tess be more like Carla, who was friendly and homey? Oh well, Carla seemed to have gotten the personality and Tess the looks. Carla was a bit on the chunky side, but then again, she'd had three kids. Tess was simply too hot for words. At work, she dressed so boringly professional in those business suits, that he was never able to see just how good she looked, but tonight . . .*wow*.

"So Teresita tells me you stole half this account from her. She was pretty upset."

Logan leaned back on the counter. "And here I thought she stole it from me."

Carla shot him an amused glance. "She must be pretty good."

Logan winked. "She's a tiger. She's cost me quite a few accounts since she started, but I'm better, and by the end of this trip, she'll know it."

Carla loaded the last dish into the dishwasher, poured grains of soap into the cavity, locked the door in place, snapped on the machine, and faced Logan squarely. "Why do you have to be better?"

"I just am."

"Don't underestimate my sister, Logan."

"I wouldn't do that."

"Teresa told me who you are, but I still invited you to dinner because I wanted to see for myself the man my sister would like to see in a coffin."

Logan laughed. "That's putting it mildly."

"Putting what mildly?" Teresa returned, a pair of sweats now covering her legs. Logan was disappointed. She'd sizzled in those cut-offs.

Both Logan and Carla flashed each other a brief look. Carla looked uncomfortable, which could only mean Tess wouldn't appreciate her big sister warning her co-worker about her. But he decided to be honest. "That you're still pouting about losing the Patagonia account."

"I'm not pouting, and I didn't lose the account."

Logan pulled away from the kitchen counter. As he passed by her on his way to the living room, he whispered close to her enticing neck, "Half—you lost half."

"You admit it, then."

He paused and looked back at her.

"If I lost it, that means you realize it was my account. I deserved it, and you stole half of it undeservedly, as you do most accounts."

Logan's earlier feeling of gloat evaporated. How dare she tell him he didn't deserve the account? He'd been doing this job twice as long as she had. He had more contacts who only wanted to do business with him. If she's had to work hard to get her buys, it wasn't his fault. He wanted to deliver the sharp reality to her, but thought better of it. They'd be spending too much time together in the next few weeks, and it would be better to attempt a truce.

"If it's any consolation, Tess, Edward did say you were his first choice, but for some reason, one of us wasn't enough. All we can do now is make sure we get the account. If we don't, the whole conversation is pointless."

"We'll get it. *I'll* get it."

Logan smiled, boy he'd like to bring her down a notch or two. It was childish, probably spurred on by male ego, but all the same, he couldn't stop himself. He gawked at her, letting his eyes settle on her breasts. He arched an eyebrow. "No doubt, Tess. You have qualities which I could never compete with, and which will certainly impress those Latin men down there who have been staring at sheep for the past three months."

He left the kitchen before she could respond. The shocked, then contemptuous expression on her noble face was enough.

CHAPTER FOUR

Teresa whirled on her sister. "Ahhrg, I hate that man. Why did you have to invite that childish, infuriating, egotistical—?"

"Calm down. The veins in your neck are going to explode."

"Carla, you just don't know him."

"I don't have to, I know you. You're too competitive. It's over—your boss made his decision, so work with the guy. With his looks, that shouldn't be such a sacrifice."

Teresa treated her sister to an impatient glare, and Carla shrugged.

"All right, all right. All I'm saying is, what choice do you have?"

"None."

"That's right."

"I wanted it so bad, though, Carla. I wanted to help Mom and Dad with the debts from that restaurant. If they lose it . . ." She shook her head, not wanting to think of their parents losing their livelihood. They still had to put the boys through school, and keep them fed and clothed. Teenagers were expensive.

"We both want to help them, Teresita. Just do what you can. Together, we won't let them lose *El Horno*."

The women went to the living room where the men were watching a Mexican soccer game.

"Watch Luis, watch Luis," Roberto pointed excitedly to the TV screen. "He practically dances with the ball."

Luis made a goal, and Roberto and the kids yelled, *Goal!* at the top of their lungs, laughing and jumping up and down.

"Let's go, Roberto," Carla said when they calmed down. "Teresita has to be up early tomorrow."

"Ah, come on, Logan wants to see the rest of it."

"Some other time," Carla insisted, gathering her kids and lining them up at the front door.

Roberto shook Logan's hand. "Well, amigo, my woman has spoken. We'll watch a whole game when you get back."

"I'll pick you up at six A.M. tomorrow, Teresa," Carla called from the front door.

"Oh, are you driving her to the airport?" Logan asked.

"Yes, that way she won't have to leave her car there."

"Mind if I tag along? I can leave my car here, can't I Tess?"

Teresa didn't know how to say no. Logically, it made sense. Why make him drive his car all the way to LAX if she was already going? But Logan brought out an evil streak in her. "I have quite a bit of luggage. I don't know that you and your bags will fit in Carla's car."

"What are you talking about, Teresa?" Roberto grumbled. "She can take the van. There's plenty of room."

"Oh." She was downright depressed. "In that case, okay."

Logan's white teeth flashed, his grin another defiant symbol that he'd won.

Everyone went out to the porch. Her sister's family climbed into their car and drove away.

Teresa and Logan waved goodbye, looking strangely like a happy couple in a disturbing horror film when everything appears normal right before the tension increases and a sinister figure jumps out at them.

Logan sat on her porch steps. *What was he doing?* She was going inside to go to sleep, so why was he making himself comfortable on her steps? He rested his forearms on his knees. "Thanks for dinner."

"I don't know what you're up to, Logan, but I'd appreciate it if you didn't come over unannounced again."

"I just came over to bring you your tickets."

Tickets she could have printed herself or accessed on her phone. "Then you decided to stay and spy on my family."

He looked at her as if she'd lost her mind. "Why would I want to do that? Carla invited me to dinner and I accepted. That was all there was to it."

He stood, moving into her personal space. He seemed larger, more muscular, more *man* than ever before.

"You could have had dinner with your family." She forced the words out of her mouth, but they held none of the earlier anger or indignation; in fact, she felt small for saying it.

"Yeah? What makes you so sure about that? Not everyone has your type of family, Tess."

He gazed at her with those puppy-dog brown eyes, making it impossible to turn away from him. She was hypnotized by the deep brown; it was warm, comforting, gentle. His pupils were large to compensate for the lack of light on the porch. Teresa managed to look down at her feet. "I was a terrible hostess. I apologize, but you caught me by surprise. You weren't exactly someone I expected would drop by."

"Loneliness makes people do strange things sometimes, I guess." He shrugged, then did something that really surprised her. He brushed the side of her face with the back of his hand so softly, so intimately, that Teresa had an urge to grab hold of that hand and direct it to roam further along her body.

Loneliness? She never pictured him as lonely. He had too much of a reputation to be left alone for long. For just a second, she felt a strange emptiness and wanted to fuse her soul to his.

***

Logan left without another word, and Teresa stood rooted where she was long after he'd driven away, an awkward feeling inside. Logan wasn't the sort of man she was attracted to. His playful style, lack of seriousness, flirtatious manner—none of that interested her in the least. But tonight, she'd witnessed a different side of him. There was this shimmer of something deeper within him that made her insides flutter when he trained those brown eyes on her. This was, perhaps, what others saw in him.

But he was the enemy. She had to keep that in mind at all times. He, like always, was standing in the way of her career goals, and this time, depriving her of the monetary reward she so badly needed to help her parents. Logan might be able to turn on that good-boy charm and dazzle people with his seductive looks, but she wouldn't let it affect her. She was too smart to fall for his games.

He sped away from Teresa's house with all his windows down. He was crazy, he was completely and absolutely insane. Who cares if Teresa could put Cindy Crawford to shame, if her wild copper hair, thick lips and tight, trim body turned him into Jell-O inside and iron outside. She hated his guts, always did, and always would. He had no business getting all wound up over her.

He had been outraged when Edward suggested they take the account together. He worked alone and didn't need a partner, much less a partner like Teresa who would bust his balls every chance she got. For a few seconds in Edward's office, he thought she might not take the job since it included working over the holidays, but although she didn't look pleased about it, she'd accepted their fate.

He braked for the stop-and-go traffic, which was a fact of life, no matter what time you got on the freeway these days. He noticed his fingers absently tapping on the steering wheel as he waited for stalled traffic to move, and he gripped the wheel tighter. He might as well accept what was going to happen and make the best of it. He'd work with Teresa, but in the end, they would approach and close the deal his way. He knew more than she did, he was better, he was senior, he was the man. . . .

As far as her personally, well, he'd treat her like he did every other female. He'd turn on the charm, be as flirtatious as he could stand it, and maybe, just maybe, it wouldn't be pure torture to be around her. He had never actually tried to melt that ice in her heart. She was a woman after all, and they all responded to him.

Traffic began rolling again, and Logan felt some tension leave him. Yes, maybe he could soften her up a bit. It definitely wouldn't be a sacrifice to try. If fact, it would be harder to try and keep his eyes and hands off her than it would be to do what came naturally and attempt to seduce her.

Traffic moved at normal speed, and Logan sat back, prepared to drive the rest of the way home with ease. This trip to Patagonia suddenly had even more appeal. He might be able to come home with not only the biggest, most profitable account yet, but with Teresa Romero wrapped around his little finger.

CHAPTER FIVE

G etting to Buenos Aires was a long, exhausting adventure in and of itself, but with Logan it became an agonizing test of patience for Teresa.

He showed up at her home as the sun was just stretching over the horizon. He loaded his and Teresa's bags into Carla's van, enthusiastically telling both women about the research he'd done on Argentina and what he hoped to see.

At the airport, he insisted on taking control. He assumed responsibility for their airline tickets and passports, checking them both in, ignoring her protests. On the plane, she had to sit beside him for eighteen torturous hours—although watching him sleep beside her was somewhat appealing. His long eyelashes flecked over his high cheekbones and curled at the ends. At the corners of his eyes, little crevices were softened. His lips, normally thinly stretched out into a smile, were pink and moist. His light brown hair was slightly rumpled. The shadow of unshaven whiskers surfaced on his face. The intimate appearance of her co-worker made her lay her head back and sigh.

When his eyelashes fluttered and his lids opened, it was too late to turn around and pretend she wasn't watching him, so she stayed put and continued to stare. He looked at her through half-open lids for what seemed like hours. In reality, only a few seconds passed.

"Can't sleep?" Logan whispered in a deep, groggy voice.

"Not on a plane."

"Want to lay your head on my shoulder?"

Teresa smiled despite herself. It was two A.M., the soft hum of the jet engines was the only sound, the plane was dark, and at the moment, Logan didn't seem so threatening. "I don't think that would help me sleep any better."

"Maybe not, but you might enjoy it just the same."

Teresa rolled her head to face away from him. "Don't worry about me, Logan. You sleep."

"Will you watch over me some more?"

Teresa faced him again, about to deny she'd watched him at all, but instead she nodded. "I might. When you're asleep is about the only time you're not being obnoxious."

Logan's lips twitched slightly. "Awe, Tess, when you say such sweet things to me, I get this tight feeling right here." He tapped his chest with his thumb. Then he crossed his arms and focused more awake eyes on her. "Why do you hate me so much?"

Teresa was floored. She wasn't used to such straightforward questions, especially not at this hour of the morning. Anyhow, she didn't hate him, not exactly, and she stated as much.

"Oh yes you do. You hate my guts. So, tell me why—let's be honest."

Teresa shifted in her seat to face him better. He watched her, a sincere look on his face as he waited for her response.

"For starters, I dislike when you play dumb. You know exactly why we don't get along."

"Because I get better accounts than you."

"Because you don't deserve to get them."

"How do you know? You've never seen me work." He leaned closer to her.

"Precisely. I've never seen you work. You spend half the time you're in the office flirting and chatting."

He half-smiled. "Is it the flirting or chatting that bothers you, or is it that I don't do it with you?"

Her indignation consumed what little tiredness she felt. She was fully awake now. "It's not fair that you waste so many business hours playing when the rest of us are working our rears off." She ignored his comment, which was meant to provoke her.

"Maybe I only need half the time to complete my work. It's not my fault if it takes you twice as long to do your job."

Teresa straightened. "How dare you—"

"Hey." He took hold of her hand and leaned over so close that she was pressed against the plane window. "Quiet down, people are trying to sleep."

Teresa wanted to shove him away, but he held her hand tight. "Move back, Logan," she warned.

"Why do you have to get so upset? We're just talking here."

"You're deliberately baiting me."

"Because it's so damn easy."

She pulled her hand loose and slammed her elbow on the wall. "Ah, damn it! See what you made me do?"

He smiled, which irritated her further. "You should have let me hold your hand. It would have been much less painful."

She glared at him as she rubbed her elbow. "See what I mean? That drives me crazy. Do you have to flirt with every female you see?"

"Now, why does that bother you so much?"

Why indeed, it wasn't any of her business. "It only bothers me because you do it to get what you want. You use that sexy smile to win over the secretaries, receptionists, mail clerk, everyone."

"You think I have a sexy smile, Tess?" he whispered, his voice thick and alluring at this hour, and his warm breath seductive as it touched her shoulder.

"Is that all you heard?" He was so exasperating.

His hand slid back and forth on her leg. "Know what I think? I think it *does* bother you that I don't flirt with you."

Did he really think she wanted his sexual attentions? She lifted his hand off her lap, and he quickly flipped it, catching her hand in his again.

"Logan, you don't flirt with me because there's nothing you want from me. The day you begin flirting, I'll know something's up."

He pulled her arm and placed her hand on *his* knee. "Maybe it'll mean I'm attracted to you and want to get you in my bed."

"Let go of my hand, Logan. You're not being funny."

"The reason I've never flirted with you is because you've placed a 'do not touch' sign on your forehead about as big as the Grand Canyon. It's not because I don't find you attractive, because I do."

"Wonderful," she said sarcastically, and even though it came out exactly as she'd intended, his words sent an unexpected thrill that reached all the way to her toes.

He smiled and released her hand, then he eased back into his own seat again. "It's true, Tess, and like you said, I have nothing to gain by saying it if it wasn't so."

"I suppose I should feel flattered." But what she felt was threatened. She didn't want those big doe eyes noticing her, not when they were expected to spend so many days together in the coming weeks.

He shrugged. "I don't much like your personality, though, even if your body's out of this world."

"You're a pig."

Logan's eyes lifted, dispassionately facing the movie screen on the seat in front of him, neither agreeing with nor denying her statement. Some passengers had their headsets on and were watching the movie. Logan watched for so long, she thought maybe their conversation was over. Amazingly, she didn't want it to be.

"So, what have you done with your kids?" That was something else she disliked about him, perhaps the most serious thing. He brought those little children to work often, making them sit quietly while he worked. He often left early because of the kids or came in late. If a woman did that, she'd be fired, but all Logan got were sympathetic looks from both men and women alike. And he drank it up, commiserating with the ladies about how difficult it was to be a single parent.

He gave her a bored expression. "My kids?"

"Yes, have you forgotten you have them already?"

"I don't have children. Are you referring to my sister's kids?"

"The little boy and girl you bring to work."

He nodded. "My sister's."

Teresa could barely hide her surprise. "I assumed they were yours. Why do you always have them with you?"

"To help Karen out. She's a single mom."

"Where's their dad?"

He frowned. "Their dad is a loser. He left Karen after Andy was born, and he comes around whenever he feels like it. I think it's when he wants a warm meal and a place to crash for the night. I'm the only constant father figure they have."

"No wonder they're always in the office," she said almost to herself.

He gave her an annoyed sideways glance. "I pick them up from school, take them in the morning, do the homework thing, you know? It helps Karen out and makes the kids feel like they have a father. Although I'm a poor substitute."

But a substitute nonetheless. "It's very kind of you."

He raised an eyebrow. "Was that a compliment?"

"I guess it was," Teresa agreed. "Not everyone would sacrifice their life, their time, for their family."

He shrugged. "You would, Tess."

She nodded, meeting his eyes in shared compassion. "Yes, you're right, I would."

He settled down into his seat, opening his legs wider in an attempt to get comfortable in the cramped airplane seat with no leg room. His knee settled against hers. He closed his eyes. "Good night."

Teresa closed her eyes also, not to sleep but to rest. She hated to admit it, but she'd gained a new respect for Logan. He wasn't a lousy father fitting his kids in around his work schedule, he was a kind, loving uncle enriching the children's lives by being a male role model.

It didn't change the fact that he was allowed to come in late whenever he wanted or bring children to work when no one else was, but somehow the way he generously gave his spare time to his family, endeared him to her.

***

When Logan awoke the next morning, he resumed his arrogant, know-it-all attitude, although it didn't bother Teresa much since once they landed, they were in a foreign country, at the mercy of other people's goodwill. Teresa did the talking, Logan the leading.

They took a taxi to the Buenos Aires port, where they boarded the cruise ship they would be on for a week.

Teresa found her cabin and dropped on her bed, exhausted and relieved to finally be in a horizontal position. She was just nodding off when she heard a knock on the door and Logan's voice outside. Grunting, she slid off the bed and yanked open the door. What do you want?"

"Want to go eat?"

"Eat? You came to bother me to go eat?"

He shrugged and looked confused. "Yeah, you barely ate that airplane food."

"Look, Logan, I'm going to climb into that bed, go to sleep, and I don't even want to see you until at least tomorrow afternoon. I don't care what you do until then."

He frowned. "Jeez, all right, just trying to be nice."

"I appreciate it," she said, sounding much more sarcastic than she meant. "Really, I do. I'm just exhausted."

***

The next day, she saw nothing of Logan. She didn't really sleep in all morning and afternoon, but she did rise late. After breakfast, she strolled around the outside ship decks, checking out where everything was. Large sparkling pools and jacuzzies were on three of the decks. Teresa made a mental note to return to them.

The inside of the ship reminded her of the time her father had taken her and Carla to the ritzy Bonaventure Hotel in Los Angeles to see how the rich people lived. Just like the hotel, every fountain, every sculpture and painting was of the highest quality. And just like when she was a kid, she felt she didn't really belong here, not yet.

She was sure she'd run into Logan at some point, but she didn't. Returning to her cabin to work, she pulled her notes out of her briefcase and began preparing the strategy for making the wool buy.

At six o'clock, Logan knocked on her door. "Did you have enough time to recover?"

"Come in." She moved aside, allowing him to enter her small, closet-sized cabin. "I've been working on the account."

He plopped on her bed. "Already? I worked on my suntan today, met a couple of cute British women, and swam in the pool."

Teresa stared at him, speechless. What do you reply to that? Good for you. "Well, tomorrow I'll show you a couple of my ideas. Now, it's dinner time, right?"

"Yep." He stood. "That's why I came for you, *darling*." He did a poor imitation of the British accent and held out his arm. "Shall we?"

"I still need to dress."

"Go ahead." He sat back down on her bed as if he were ready to watch a good movie.

Teresa put a hand on her hip. "Out, Wilde, wait outside."

He snapped his fingers and made a face as if he were greatly disappointed. "Damn, I get in a woman's cabin and get kicked out the first night." He went out good-naturedly, and Teresa couldn't help but smile. He was just too much.

Logan looked terrific in his dinner tux, and although he always dressed well, she was impressed.

Teresa wore her strapless black evening gown she'd bought two years ago for a New Year's Eve party her then-boyfriend dragged her to. Logan eyed her appreciatively when she walked out of her cabin door. "Not bad, Tess. Definitely worth the wait."

Their elegant dinner table made her feel like she and Logan were on a date, and it was somewhat disconcerting. Logan bought a bottle of Argentine Malbec for them to share, and Teresa tried not to notice the way his eyes stayed glued to her lips as she sipped from her wine goblet. Three other couples arrived and introduced themselves.

"Are you together?" An elderly lady, named Betty asked.

"Yes," Logan said, beaming at Teresa.

She gave him a tight smile back. They were *not* together. Not the way the woman meant. But she let it pass.

They ate a marvelous prime rib and crab dinner decorated with baby carrots, broccoli and cauliflower. And after the full meal, luscious dessert choices were presented.

"What does your husband do?" Betty asked Teresa about Logan.

"He's not my husband." Teresa decided to correct the misconception before it continued the rest of the week.

"I see." The woman looked at her disapprovingly. Teresa realized she didn't see at all. Logan had already said they were together, and to deny being married didn't deny a relationship—Teresa had only implicated herself further. She decided it didn't really matter what these people believed.

The waiters brought out the decadently rich chocolate mousse she ordered and thick, dark coffee. Since morning, the ship seemed to have picked up speed, and either the swaying had intensified or the exhaustion was catching up to her because she was starting to feel queasy. Teresa had a couple of bites of the mousse, then decided against putting anything else in her stomach that might not stay down very long.

Logan covered her hand. "You okay?"

She didn't pull her hand away from the warm, intimate gesture. "I don't think so."

He wiped his mouth with the linen napkin, which rested properly on his lap. "We're going to head back to our staterooms a little early. Nice to have met you all," he said to their table companions.

They all smiled and nodded and returned the pleasantries. Teresa stood, said goodbye, and walked alongside Logan. "I could have left alone."

"I was finished eating. I'll walk you to your room." It seemed as if he were going to take her hand, but at the last moment changed his mind. He pressed the heel of his palm on her lower back for just a second as he guided her into the elevator.

Teresa noticed how fluid he moved, even on a rocking ship. He got them to her appropriate deck, took her key, opened her door, and followed her inside. For once, she was grateful for his controlling behavior because the minute she reached the inside of her cabin, she rushed to the bathroom where her dinner came heaving out. Afterward, her head was splitting and her forehead was beaded with sweat. She washed her face with cold water. At least the nausea was gone.

"Hey, Tess, can I come in?"

"No." She heard him standing outside the bathroom door. "I'll be right out."

She swayed out of the bathroom, holding on to the walls for support. Her legs felt like rubber. Logan's brows were low above his eyes, his forehead heavily creased. "I didn't know you got seasick."

"Neither did I."

"Come on." He pulled her toward the bed, supporting her half-limp body against his. She noticed he'd pulled the sheets back. He patted her pillow. "Lie down."

Teresa looked at his concerned puppy dog eyes. She felt her stomach heave again, but the ship had stopped rocking. "I can handle it from here, Logan. Thanks."

He gripped her forearm. "Just rest for a few minutes. You can get up and change when I leave."

She did as he asked.

Logan crouched down beside her and smiled. "Not my idea of how I wanted to get you into bed, but there you go."

She smiled. "Knowing you, I'm sure you'll tell everyone you did."

He laughed, too loud for her pounding head. "Now, there's an idea." He slid damp hair off her forehead. His frown reappeared. "Can I get you anything?"

She shook her head. "I'll be okay. I think I just need to sleep."

He nodded and dropped a kiss on her forehead as if she were a child. Then he bolted up. "See you tomorrow, Tiger."

Logan knew he was playing with fire. That woman would love nothing better than to string him up to one of the cactuses outside their offices and watch him slowly bleed to death. So why the heck was he noticing how her bottom swayed as she walked to the dining room tonight? And why had his crotch begun growing to the point he had to practically run out of her stateroom? He lay back on the sun deck, cradling his head in his hands, and stared up at the multitude of stars. A cool breeze blew as the ship made its slow trek south. He began to count the stars, which was an infinitely better idea than trying to examine why his brain knew what was good for him, but his body did not. He sighed. Being a man was just plain hard . . . if only women understood that. From now on, he had to make a concerted effort to stick to business with her. Either that or sleep with her.

CHAPTER SIX

Not once, but three times, Teresa went to Logan's room, knocked, and got no answer. She glanced at her watch impatiently. Three P.M. She didn't know what was wrong with him. This was the second day he'd left her to do all the work herself. He didn't answer his cell, or it wasn't working. She left a note that she'd be getting a drink at the Signature Lounge.

She'd worked all morning, feeling much better. Her body had finally accepted the constant swaying. Last night, Logan had been so kind, tending to her. He'd actually looked concerned. She was embarrassed he'd seen her like that, but he'd helped her, made her feel better, and hadn't made a big deal about it. For that, she was grateful.

"Hey beautiful. Thanks for the invite." Logan looked tan, relaxed, gorgeous.

"Where have you been?"

"I'll have what she's having," he said to the cocktail waiter, then smiled at her. "Lets see. I swam, ate breakfast, read a few chapters of a mystery novel, lost some money in the casino, ate lunch, read some more, and now here I am, having a drink with you. Good idea by the way."

"Logan, did you forget we're here to work?"

His eyes widened as if she'd said she was jumping ship. "You're kidding, right?"

"No, I'm not kidding. We only have about four more days before we get to San Julian."

"And?"

"And we should have a united, strategic plan to present them at the farm. We can't just show up and not know what we want."

He lifted the drink placed before him and looked at her as if she were stupid. "We know what we want—wool."

"Logan, you know what I mean."

He took a sip, then scrunched up his face. "What the hell is this?"

"Hot chocolate and cherry brandy."

"Ugh, it's disgusting."

Teresa reached across, took it out of his hand, and handed him a glass of water. "You shouldn't order things you don't know."

"I didn't know you had such strange tastes. No wonder you got sick yesterday." He ordered a Singapore Sling as if that were much better. She finished her drink and started on his chocolate and cherry brandy.

He placed his hand on her knee as he'd done on the airplane. "Here's the plan. I thought about it last night as I counted the stars—"

"As you counted the stars?"

"Don't ask. Here's what we do. We tell them how we've studied the sheep farms around the world—U.S., Australia, Chile, Argentina—and that out of all the ones we've seen, we've picked them. They get to be the suppliers of a major U.S. clothing company. What else can they ask for? *And* because we're so nice, we're even going to write them a big fat check." He gulped a huge amount of his drink and faced her with a satisfied smile.

"Oh, that's brilliant, Logan. Why didn't I think of that myself?"

He shrugged and drank more. Apparently, this man never learned to nurse his drink. "Have you considered, even for a second, what you'll do when they laugh in your face and put you on the first ship back to Buenos Aires?"

He leaned back in his seat. "That's where you come in."

"Oh?" He had her full attention now.

He nodded. "Ahhm, this is where you put on the tightest jeans you can fit into and an equally tight shirt to emphasize those nice, hmmm . . ." He cleared his throat and smiled.

Teresa did not smile.

"Or" —he straightened—"that was a bad idea. We go with your plan, which you've been diligently putting together."

"You see what I mean? You don't have a clue. I don't know what Edward Reed was thinking sending you down for such an important account."

He finished his drink, put his arm around her shoulder, and pulled her so close she smelled the citrusy alcohol on his breath. "I'll tell you what he was thinking. This cruise was our reward for doing a good job for him. He wanted us to enjoy it and worry about work when we get to San Julian. So relax, have a few more of those medicine hot chocolates, and soon you'll forget all about sheep and wool."

She lifted his heavy arm off her. "You're pitiful. You'll be drunk before dinner."

He lifted his glass in the air. "I certainly hope so."

Teresa got up, frustrated from trying to reason with a man who acted worse than a child. She couldn't believe he was going to let her do all the work, then take half the credit for it.

He snatched up her wrist. "Get drunk with me, Tess. Let's have a good time. Forget you hate me for the rest of the cruise at least."

She looked up at his handsome face to find a disquieting, pleading look in his eyes. "I don't hate you, Logan. But getting drunk with you is not my idea of a good time, sorry."

He released her wrist and ordered another Singapore Sling. "You don't have the slightest idea how to have a good time, Tessa, baby." He winked and sat back to drain his new drink.

Teresa left him in the lounge. Just when she was starting to like him, he reminded her why she didn't.

##

It became increasingly difficult to work as she'd planned. The next morning, they docked at their first port of Mar Del Plata, and she didn't have to actually see Logan disembarking to know he'd be getting off to sightsee. It seemed he was on vacation. Teresa worked until midday then curiosity got the best of her, and she went to the sun deck to lie out and look at the spectacular beach city. The sun was bright and warm, and slow-floating cumulus clouds floated overhead, producing periods of relief from the hot sun. Teresa ordered lunch out on deck, enjoying the feeling of being outdoors and being waited on. After a couple of hours, she felt guilty and returned to her room to finish her reading on Argentina's sheep industry.

Logan didn't come for her at dinner time, and she wondered if maybe she actually had offended him. She dressed and went to dinner and found him at the table when she got there. The other couples still had not arrived. His grand smile told her he was not angry. She hadn't thought so. He wasn't the type to hold grudges.

"Good time out on port?"

"Oh, terrific, you should have come, Tess."

"I actually had quite an enjoyable time aboard ship. I sat out in the sun for a while. The view was beautiful." She didn't want him to think he was the only one having fun.

He raised both eyebrows. "Good for you. Maybe there's hope for you after all." He poured them both wine and lifted his glass. "Cheers."

"*Salud*." She lifted her own goblet, feeling a shaky peace had been reached somehow, although she couldn't say how or why she felt that way.

##

The next day Logan actually came to her stateroom after breakfast and asked to see what she'd prepared. They spent all day talking shop. He irritated her by telling her she was wrong on a couple of approaches. They discussed it quite vigorously. He conceded on one point, she on another.

They called room service for lunch, and stacks of turkey, and ham and cheese sandwiches arrived with a platter of fresh fruit. Logan sat on Teresa'bed against the wall, his legs stretched out and crossed at the ankles. Teresa wondered how it was possible for a person to look so at ease all the time.

"Maybe," he said, taking a bite, chewing, and swallowing. "They'll be happy to sell us their wool, and none of this will be an issue."

Teresa sat at the small desk beside the bed, adding mayonnaise to her sandwich. "Maybe, but I doubt it, they're already working with local retailers, and they don't have any of the problems of international taxes or dealing with government red tape."

Logan took a few more bites. The lines on his forehead told her he was considering what she'd said. "I think this is the best sandwich I've had in a long time."

Teresa was about to bite into hers, but she stopped and looked at him. She'd expected him to say something brilliant about acquiring the wool, and instead, he was only enjoying his food. She bit into her sandwich. It *was* good. "It's possible that they may go for the compromise of sharing the cost of their taxes. That way, the burden isn't completely on them."

"I think it's the ham that makes it so flavorful. It's like Black Forest, isn't it?"

Teresa glanced at her sandwich, then returned it to her plate. She sipped her diet coke as she sank deeper into her chair. "Of course, the draw of being associated with a major U.S. company could be all the incentive they'll need."

"Hey, Teresa, you think you'll ever have kids?"

"What?"

"Kids. You want some?"

She stared at him, blinked, and wondered what brought about that question. She felt her cheeks warm. "Sure, someday. Why?"

"Do you think they'll have your cute curved nose, or your cinnamon hair, or that creamy coffee color skin or—"

"Logan, what the heck are you talking about? How should I know what they'll look like?"

"So, there's no point in discussing it, is there?"

"No, so—"

"Just like there's no point in trying to guess what deal the Estancia owner will go for."

She twisted her lips in disapproval. "Cute, but it's not the same thing."

He slid off the bed and placed his plate on the desk. "It's exactly the same thing. You're talking hypothetically, Tess. We won't know until we get there what they're expecting. The only thing we know for sure is that they're interested, or they wouldn't have told Edward to send us. When we get there, we'll see what their expectations are, and we'll ask for a few days to think about it. Then we'll counter offer or accept."

"But don't you think we'll be better prepared to counter if we've thought of the various scenarios ahead of time?"

"It won't make a bit of difference."

She disagreed, but she let it go.

"Gonna finish your sandwich?" He sat in front of her, eyeing her plate like a hungry puppy dog.

Teresa shook her head. "I'm full."

He smiled. "Can I have it?"

Sitting alone in the small cabin, sharing her food with him as she might with friends and family, created an intimacy she wasn't entirely comfortable with. She handed him her plate without a word. He grabbed it and took large bites as if his hunger were unrelenting.

Logan's passion for life was evident in the intensity he experienced everything, even the way he enjoyed his food. Suddenly, Teresa's own appetite returned. She took an apple from the fruit bowl, grabbed her sunglasses, and decided to go on deck to enjoy the rest of the afternoon sun.

"Where are you going?" Logan looked surprised.

"Outside."

"All right!" He wiped the mayonnaise from the corner of his lips and followed her. But as he reached the door, he made a 180-degree turn, grabbed his own apple and a banana, and then went back out.

CHAPTER SEVEN

S he climbed to the sun deck, then discarded all her clothes except for a light blue bikini, which accentuated her flaring hips and thrusting breasts. She spread her luscious body out on a deck chair under the bright sun.

"What?" She frowned.

"What do you mean, what?"

"You're staring."

"Oh, ah . . ." He sat beside her and continued to admire her curves. "The blue bikini looks good on you."

"It's teal."

"Is it?" He rubbed his chin, thinking teal was the most wonderful color he'd ever seen.

She shook her head just like the senior high-school girls did in school when the lowly scrubs hit on them. Then she lay back and ignored him. Logan went to the Sun Shop and bought suntan lotion. It might be an obvious ploy to get a cheap feel, but what the heck.

When he strolled back, Tess looked like she might be asleep. Since she couldn't see him and act annoyed, he stared openly. Her hip bones were prominent, and a deep, hollow valley extended between her ribs and pelvic bone. Carla was right; Tess was too thin. Her legs were long and well-shaped, though, and her breasts looked firm and overflowed the large cup size. He sat beside her, squirted the cool lotion into the palm of his hands, rubbed them together, then slathered it on her thigh. She jerked her head up immediately.

"Just me, sorry."

"What do you think you're doing?"

"Preserving your skin. Too much sun isn't good for you."

"Logan, I'm out here to get tanned."

"Exactly, so you don't want to burn. Lay back, relax."

She gazed at him suspiciously for a few more seconds, then slowly lowered herself back again. Logan almost cheered. She wasn't going to protest. He massaged the lotion around her calves, going higher up her leg each time, taking considerable time on her thighs.

"Careful, Logan," she warned through closed eyes.

He smiled even though she wasn't looking at him. He ignored her warning, lifted her legs, and applied the suntan balm on her inner thighs in soft circular motions meant to arouse her. She didn't so much as move a muscle.

Then he squirted the scented, white cream on her belly. She gasped, and he saw her stomach muscles clench. He rubbed in the lotion, up and down her rib cage and around her hollow belly. "Don't you eat?" He asked.

"Of course I eat."

Did he imagine it, or was her voice huskier than usual? "You're so thin."

"I don't think so."

He didn't imagine it. Her voice was thicker and shakier. Maybe he was getting through her icy shell after all. He rubbed his fingers between her breasts. She opened her eyes and held his in her gaze. Her face was flushed. "Are you hot?" he asked.

"It's warm."

"I'll do your shoulders and then your back, if you'd like."

Teresa wanted to die. Why was she letting this irritating man rub his hands all over her body? Of course, she knew why. She hadn't wanted to appear childish or prudish, after all, all he was doing was putting lotion on her skin, so she'd stupidly submitted.

His fingertips moved softly, caressingly, on the tops of her breasts and cleavage. She wanted to shove his hand away, but then he'd know the effect his touch was creating inside her.

"No," she said. "My back and shoulders will be fine."

"Don't be silly. You'll burn if I don't apply it to your back. Go on, turn over."

"Fine." She flipped over just to turn away from him and avoid the embarrassment of looking into his eyes.

His warm, heavy hand slid along her back, his fingers pressing on the indentation of her spine. Then he pulled on the strap of her bikini top, and it came undone.

"Logan!"

"I'll tie it back up when I'm done. Why are you so uptight?"

"You're undressing me."

He chuckled. "Me? You're the one who stripped down to nothing. Not that I'm complaining."

He continued to run his lotion-smoothed hands along her back and shoulders, although the lotion had already seeped into her skin.

"All right, Logan, that's enough."

He leaned over her. His chest t shielded the heat from the sun, but generated its own heat. The scent of his cologne overpowered the tropical smell of lotion on her skin. "Are you sure, Tess?" His voice was above her right ear.

She couldn't get up and push him away without flashing her breasts to everyone on deck, but when she got the top fastened, she was going to kill him. "Tie me back up."

Both hands settled on her back, and he slowly, methodically, began making a bow with the skimpy strings, while he nuzzled the back of her neck with his lips. Then, all of a sudden, he spanked her bottom and stood. "All done."

She flipped over as quickly as he jumped back. "You low life, come back here."

He grinned quite handsomely. "You sure do look good all oiled up in that 'teal' suit."

"You think you're cute, don't you?"

He shrugged. "Pretty much." He came closer and dared to sit beside her again. "You're not really upset, are you? I was just having a little fun."

How could you strangle someone who willingly stuck his neck in your hands? "At my expense." She adjusted the back of the lounge chair and reclined against it.

"All right, I admit it. It gave me a cheap thrill to touch you. Did you enjoy it, just a little?"

"No!" She lied. It felt wonderful.

"Oh well." He shrugged again. "I tried. No damage done then. Put some on me?"

Pleading puppy dog eyes were again aimed at her. He was pitiful, but somewhat adorable. She snatched the bottle of lotion, angry at herself for reacting to his teasing.

"Turn around." She snapped out the words and pretended it was a great sacrifice, but actually, smoothing the lotion on his taut, wide shoulders was rather pleasurable.

When she finished, he offered a charming smile. "Thank you, sweetheart. You did a great job."

Teresa handed him back his bottle, ignoring his Hollywood performance for heartthrob.

"What about my chest and legs?"

What about them? She was finished touching him. "You can reach those areas yourself."

"I can, sure, but I'd rather you did it. Unlike you, I can admit that I enjoyed your hands caressing my body."

She was really becoming bothered by all this. She knew he was teasing her, but she wasn't used to these types of games. She refused to answer him anymore.

He laughed under his breath. "Well, you can run your hands up and down my body anytime you want." He winked.

She closed her eyes, hoping he'd shut up.

"Hey, Tess."

She opened her eyes and glared at him.

"You okay?"

His question surprised her, but more than the question, it was the tenderness in his voice. "Sure, why wouldn't I be?"

"Because." He smiled. "I'm being a shit, but I don't mean anything by it. I like to be playful, but sometimes I get carried away."

She nodded. "I've noticed."

"We work together, and I guess I should ease up, but I'm afraid I don't really know how. I don't mean to make you uncomfortable."

She was about to deny that he had, but since he was being so honest, she smiled. "You meant to make me *very* uncomfortable."

He tilted his head and gazed at her warmly. "You're right, because you make *me* so damn uncomfortable most of the time, you know that?"

No, she didn't. "How so?" She never touched him or got in his space.

"You've got this electric shield around you, and if someone gets too close, they get zapped. You're always ready to zap me."

She averted her eyes. Was she really that mean to him? "Because you're always so obnoxious."

He shrugged. "I'm intimidated by strong women."

She laughed. Logan was intimidated by no one. "Right."

He chuckled. "You can be intimidating, Tess. Maybe I'm obnoxious around you because you make me nervous."

"Maybe, you just enjoy giving me a hard time."

His guilty, lopsided grin told her she was right. "It's fun watching you lose your cool."

"You're not nice."

His lighthearted mood changed. "And you're just plain hostile, Tess."

She frowned. No matter what she thought of him, she had no right to be rude or deny him the respect she gave every other co-worker. "I'm sorry."

He winked. "Friends?"

"It's possible." She nodded. Then she slipped on her sunglasses and sat back to relax in the sun. Luckily, he did the same, leaving her to her own confused thoughts.

CHAPTER EIGHT

L ogan was surprised at how good the day turned out. After Teresa got her fill of sun, he convinced her to play a game of Blackjack with him in the game room. Logan was amazed that she didn't know how to play such a simple game. But Teresa hadn't played cards when she was young, she explained. Her family was poor, and the kids entertained themselves by playing imaginative games.

"You didn't have toys?" Logan asked unbelievingly.

"Sure, we had some toys, but usually mom and dad bought us one toy for Christmas, and the rest of our presents were clothes we needed, or school supplies."

Logan shuffled the cards. "No one asked for cards? They're cheap."

"Would you if you only got one present a year, or would you ask for the amazing ice skating doll?"

Logan laughed. "Well, there's no question. I see your point."

He'd dealt the cards, explained the rules, and they played a few hands. Teresa caught on fast, and then of course, she began to play to win. Her competitive nature didn't just extend to work, it seemed. He enjoyed watching her get all flustered and determined to win the next hand when she lost. Her face colored to a maroon shade, which made her look even more beautiful. They played for a couple of hours, after which he dragged her to play bingo. They both lost.

What pleased him, though, was that she appeared to be having a good time. And surprisingly, he found he was enjoying her company. When they broke to change and get ready for dinner, he was actually looking forward to seeing her again.

At the dinner table, everything was decorated for Christmas. Garland hung from the chandeliers, and poinsettias seemed to adorn every empty corner of the dining room. Teresa was in high spirits, and Logan sat back and watched her interact with the other couples. He wondered what kind of woman she was on a date. He found her alluring: a strong woman with an unerring magnetism.

Maybe the excitement of trying to outwit that tumultuous personality was what drew him. It was like being at the receiving end of a wild storm—surviving, and then being taking glory from the fact you withstood it and won. He would never want to control Tess; just like a storm, it was impossible, but he wanted to take all she had to give and triumph. She was a worthy opponent in everything, even in bed, he imagined,

He found himself staring at her as she spoke animatedly about the obligation of companies to make sure their representatives didn't embarrass the firm. He speculated on the lucky man—the one she chose as a lover. Teresa would want him to be perfect—no, he would need to be exceptional. Logan wouldn't mind a match with her in bed. She turned to him then and smiled. He smiled back, feeling awkward as if she'd caught him, read his thoughts.

"Don't you agree, Logan?"

He didn't know what she'd been talking about. "Tess, we agree on so little. What do you think?"

"I think even you have to admit that if an employee makes the company he works for look bad, they should be fired."

"As usual, you're too dramatic. I don't believe in absolutes."

Teresa waved away his opinion and returned her attention to the woman beside her, who seemed to agree with whatever Tess said.

After dinner, he invited Tess to dance, but she refused. Logan was disappointed; he didn't want to say good night yet. They'd had a good day and evening. But he didn't want to seem too eager. He didn't even know why he wanted to spend more time with her anyway. "You'll miss out." He winked, his last attempt at getting her to change her mind.

She gave him a pretty smile, so natural and light that he almost lost his attempt at casualness. He realized this was the first day she hadn't been scowling at him.

"Enjoy yourself, Logan," she said. "I need some peace tonight."

He went to the dancing lounge, ordered a beer, and watched others dance, feeling no real desire to participate himself. He would have danced with Tess, but he had no urge to dance with anyone else tonight. Since he wasn't ready to sleep yet, he ordered a second beer, sat back, and enjoyed the music.

The alcohol, loud music, and smoke combined to muddy his thinking. Other Christmas Eves floated in and out of his brain. Happy times with his parents; doing last-minute wrapping in his bedroom; whipping up the eggnog with his dad and his mother warning not to make it too strong.

Logan rubbed his face with both hands. They were ghosts now. Drinking in a bar—even on a fancy cruise ship—was no way to spend Christmas Eve. He'd done that too many times, feeling sorry for himself, and punishing himself for still being alive when those he loved weren't. He paid for his beers and headed out for the promenade deck to get some fresh air. He no longer permitted himself to wallow in self-pity. It was destructive and pointless.

A few couples strolled along the teak wood deck, but what caught his eye was a shapely figure in red, Tess, standing at the rail near the front of the ship. She was looking out at the blackness of the sea, the wind blowing her hair. The heaviness in his heart began to lift. God, she looked beautiful. Disregarding the fact that she might not want his company, he quietly came up behind her. "Hypnotic, isn't it?"

She gasped and swung around so fast she swayed right into Logan's chest. He looped his arms around her waist, finding something very comforting in holding her against him. As she looked up at him, the side of her face rubbed against the side of his.

"Sorry, didn't mean to startle you," he said.

She swallowed and closed her wide eyes. He felt her relax against his chest, and it seemed so right that she should be in his arms. He knew she'd steadied herself, and he should let her go, but he wasn't stupid. He pulled her closer. "You okay?"

"Why did you sneak up behind me?" Her eyes were open again.

He slid his face down hers and touched his chin to her shoulder. Her hair smelled like strawberries. "I didn't. You must have been in deep thought."

She sighed. "I guess." She made an attempt to step out of his arms, so he tightened them and walked closer to her so they were touching at all points from their heads to their legs. "What's the matter, Tess? What are you doing out here all alone?"

If he could get her talking, then maybe she'd let him hold her a little longer. She stiffened again, but then, to his surprise, she actually leaned into him.

"You'll make fun of me if I tell you."

"I won't. I promise." Her soft hair blew on his face, as if caressing him. He began to get aroused. He tried to ignore it and concentrate instead on what she said.

"I guess I'm lonely."

He tightened his arms around her. *Me too, Tess.* But he couldn't admit that. "Yeah?"

"It's Christmas Eve, and at home I'd be with my family. My mom would have a huge turkey in the oven and we'd be snacking on tamales and chips and salsa. My dad would have Ranchera music going, and my brothers would be complaining, wanting to hear rock or rap instead."

Logan thought of Karen and the kids spending Christmas alone. He didn't want to think about it. It was too depressing. "Sounds like you guys have a lot of fun."

She nodded again, her hair tickling his face. This time, he couldn't resist; he nuzzled her neck.

"Logan, let me go."

"Why?" he whispered, needing to feel this closeness.

"You know why."

Because I'm getting a huge erection? Damn his body. Of course, she could probably feel it, but she was being polite and not saying it. "I'm sorry, I guess I'm lonely too."

She laughed. "You're pitiful. Is everything a line to you?"

He didn't want to, but he released her. He stood beside her next to the rail. "It's not a line, Tess; you think I don't miss my sister and the kids? They're all the family I have."

She looked at him strangely. "Where are your parents?"

He gazed down at the water hitting the side of the ship and watched the spray it created. Even in the dark, it was visible. "Dead," he said, not wanting to talk about himself, but she persisted.

"Both your parents? You're not that old."

He clasped his hands together in front of him. His forearms rested on the railing. "They died in a fire. Our house burned down." And it was his damn fault.

"Oh, how awful. You and your sister weren't there?"

Logan straightened. Apparently, he was too abrupt because she looked as if he'd startled her again. "No, luckily we weren't." He gave her a forced smile and took her hand. "Tell me more about your family."

She stared at him with a look of understanding. After a few moments, she smiled. "I love them. I'd do anything to keep them well and happy."

Logan entwined his fingers with hers. She glanced down at their joined hands, then continued speaking. "My dad wants me to get married and give him grandkids like my sister." She laughed as if that were an impossible idea. "But no one I date is ever good enough, so I don't know who he thinks I'm going to marry."

Logan stepped closer to her, still holding her hand. "Do you date a lot?"

"No, actually I don't, but when I do, Dad's so mean to the men, I'm surprised they don't run away the instant they meet him."

"I bet you get your temper from him." Logan teased her.

She smiled. "Yes, I'm more like him. My sister is like my mom. She cooks, likes kids—"

"You don't"

"Cook?"

"Like kids."

"Oh, sure I do, but I don't have any. That's all Carla's ever wanted since we were kids, to get married and have a family. I dreamed of having my own car, a house, and a great job."

"Looks like you both got what you wanted." Logan turned on his side, leaning his hip on the rail so he could get a better look at Teresa. She looked vulnerable and feminine tonight, and he wanted to take care of her.

"Well, *she* did anyway."

"What are you missing, Tess?"

She smiled, her full lips red and glossy. "The car, the house, and the job," she said.

"You have a good job."

"I was picturing something like CEO of a major Fortune 500 company, or at least president of my *own* company, you know?" Her smile broadened.

She had gorgeous lips. Logan smiled back. He wanted to hold her again. He wanted to kiss her. "Well, although you're not a billionaire CEO yet, you do get to work with me. That's a benefit, isn't it?"

She raised an eyebrow and shot him a warning look. "You don't really want me to answer that, do you?"

He stepped forward and looped an arm around her waist. "Yes, I do. I want you to admit I'm not the monster you made me out to be."

She began to protest his closeness, then gazed into his eyes, sending shockwaves through his body. "I may have been too quick to judge you personally. Professionally, I think I'm right on the money."

"I have a suggestion . . ."

"What?" she looked apprehensive.

"Let's forget about work for the next few days. I want to get to know you better."

She still looked unsure. "What did you have in mind?"

"This." He bowed his head and tasted her full lips. They were as velvety and lush as they looked, and Logan pulled her deeper into an embrace, greedily savoring the kiss. He parted her lips and dipped his tongue, exploring the inner softness of her mouth and meeting her tongue tentatively. She returned his kiss, not as passionately as he wished, but returned it all the same.

When he lifted his head, he noticed her eyes were clouded over, and that pleased him.

"That was nice," she whispered.

He smiled. Oh yes, he was absolutely pleased.

"But definitely a bad idea." She touched her hands to his shoulders.

No, that's not what he wanted to hear, not when he held her in his arms and knew she was enjoying it as much as he was. "Funny," he said in his sexiest voice, the tone that seemed to sway every woman he'd ever tried to seduce. "I think it's the best idea I've had in a long time."

She didn't look swayed, but she wasn't making an attempt to get away from him either. This gave him hope.

"We're co-workers, competitors even," she reasoned.

"So?"

"You think it's wise to start a relationship doomed to fall apart."

He pushed his hand into her lower back, caressing. "I think it's wise for us to have some fun. Work is work; it has nothing to do with us personally."

"It has everything to do with it."

He brought his lips to where her neck and shoulder met and kissed the soft crevice there. He wanted her, and he just decided he'd have her.

She stiffened and put pressure on his shoulders. "Logan, don't do this." Her deep voice aroused him.

"Don't think Tess, honey. This doesn't have to be complicated. Let's just enjoy each other, no strings."

The pressure on his shoulders now was a definite push, so he lifted his head and loosened his hold on her. "Sorry." He smiled.

She stepped out of his arms, and Logan was disappointed.

"I can't do that, Logan. I couldn't have, I mean, I couldn't be . . . intimate with you and continue to work together."

Logan laughed. "Why not?"

She shrugged. "We have a business relationship. It needs to stay that way. I can't mix the two."

"Don't you think that's ridiculous, Tess?"

"Sorry, I don't."

Logan took her hand. "We're together on an exotic trip, we're attracted to each other, we could make each other feel good, a little less lonely. There's nothing wrong with that, but I respect your decision. The offer will stand, though. If you want to have a good time—no pressure, no commitment—just fun, let me know." He kissed her gently on her bright red lips and winked.

She looked disoriented as he turned away from her. He left her standing where he'd found her, hoping he sounded more casual than he felt. He crossed his fingers, praying she'd take him up on his offer, not only because he wanted her, but because something told him Tess could use a simple, no-strings affair, and he wanted to be the one she had it with. He was egotistical maybe, but the pleasure, the pure ecstasy he could bring her, would be something she'd never forget.

CHAPTER NINE

T eresa closed her stateroom door and stood beside it for a few seconds. The thumping of her heart showed no sign of slowing. What had happened tonight? She turned and glanced at the full-length mirror on the closet door. She was flushed, her hair was wildly tossed from the wind, her lips were thick and red. Teresa groaned. *Look at me, I look like an open invitation.*

She walked farther into the room and sat on the bed. As she was kicking off her shoes, she heard a knock on her door. *Oh God, don't let it be Logan.*

When she cracked it open, Logan thrust his hand through, and in his fist, he held a candy cane. Teresa smiled and opened the door wider. "What are you doing, Logan? Don't you sleep?"

He smiled lazily. "It's after midnight, officially Christmas."

She checked her watch. "Why, it is."

"Can I come in?"

Her heart still raced from the last time she allowed him to get close. Letting him into her stateroom was a bad idea.

Noticing her hesitation, his smile widened. "Come on, Tess, live dangerously."

"I'm not afraid of you."

"Then it's yourself you're afraid of, huh?"

She smiled and shook her head. He was simply irresistible. "Thank you for the candy cane, it was very sweet of you to come down—"

"I've got more." He pushed the door all the way open. "It's not polite to leave me out here on Christmas morning."

She had no choice but to move back, or he would have stepped right into her. Then he pulled out a small box and offered it to her.

"What's this?" She frowned at him.

"Merry Christmas. I couldn't wait until morning, especially since you were so sad tonight."

"You bought me a gift?" She didn't know what to say. "After all the unkind things I've said to you through the years?"

"You didn't really mean any of them."

She angled her head and stared at him. She couldn't believe him. He was perceptive. No, she never meant to lash out at him. She'd been angry at an image she'd formed of Logan, not the real man. She'd even been jealous of his successes, which he seemed to attain so easily. Now, as he stood in front of her with a boyish, hopeful expression, waiting for her to open her gift, she felt foolish for every nasty thought she'd ever had about him.

"I don't know what to say. This is so sweet of you."

"Open the box."

She gazed at him for another moment, then smiled as she snapped back the black velvet lid. Inside was a pair of magnificent emerald earrings set on an S-shape gold setting. Teresa's jaw dropped in disbelief; her eyes met his. "Logan . . ."

"I figured green would be good for Christmas. Do you like them?" His eyes sparkled as much as the emeralds on the earrings.

"They're unbelievably beautiful. Where did you—?"

"Down a couple of decks at the boutique. I'm glad you like them. Merry Christmas."

She bit her bottom lip and shook her head. "This is too much. I should tell you I can't accept them."

He smiled and entered her personal space, reclaiming the box and holding it up to the side of her face. "But they'll look so good on you, you really should." He placed the box on a desk, then wrapped his arms around her waist.

"Well, thank you. I'll wear them tomorrow night."

Logan didn't move, but his lips seemed to be inching closer to hers. His warm breath doing things inside she'd only read about.

She knew he was waiting for the kiss they both wanted, but Teresa knew tonight, it wouldn't end with a kiss. Not when they were both feeling lonely and craving the touch and warmth of another. She placed her hands on his shoulders. "It could be anyone tonight, Logan," she whispered, stating the truth of her feelings. "What we're feeling isn't real."

He slid his face against hers, as Carla's cat often did against her leg. His sprouting whiskers scratched invitingly against the sensitive skin of her cheek. His lips leisurely brushed the side of her neck, sending her super-sensitive nerve-endings into overdrive. Teresa shivered and her arms encircled his neck, her fingers sliding up until they were deep in satiny strands of brown hair. She closed her eyes and stepped closer, pressing her body to his.

"But it isn't just anyone, is it?" he said hoarsely. "It's you, and it's me, and we want this, we deserve this."

She wanted to ask how he figured that, but he continued to kiss her neck, up her jaw line until he found her lips. Then like a man dying of thirst, he moaned and closed his lips over hers, mercilessly destroying every rational thought she had left.

He thrust his tongue through her lips where it met with hers. She clasped the back of his neck and allowed him to shatter her senses. He tasted of citrus, of rum, of hot desire. She wanted all of him. She felt his thickness, like iron, pressed against her abdomen. If she allowed it, it could be inside her, thrusting into her as hot and urgently as his tongue had through her lips.

Teresa broke the kiss fiercely and abruptly. She gasped for air and stepped back, but in the confining space, there was nowhere to go; the backs of her knees hit the bed, and she fell back.

Logan also took a deep breath and held out his hands, palms open, facing her as if to let her know he wouldn't invade her space. "Don't look at me like that," he dragged the words out of his throat.

She lowered her eyes. What did he see in them, fear or desire, or both? "You'd better leave before I make a fool of myself, Logan."

"Is this the 'I won't respect you in the morning' bullshit? That's a little old-fashioned, isn't it?"

She gazed at him again. Yes, old-fashioned was exactly what she was. "You don't respect me now, Logan—it's myself I have to be able to face tomorrow. Take your bribe gift and leave."

"What?" His lips tightened, and he scowled. "Look, I bought you the earrings because I wanted you to have them. And if you call wanting to throw you on that bed to make love to you 'til morning, 'disrespectful,' you're right, I don't respect you at all."

He charged out of her room, and Teresa could feel the stinging tears behind her eyes.

##

The next couple of days, she ignored Logan, deciding they needed to put some distance between them. To her annoyance, he did the same. However, achieving the desired distance on a ship was not as easy as she'd hoped. When she tried sunbathing, he ended up swimming at the nearby pool, flirting shamelessly with any woman, young or old, who happened to be around him. If she went to the library to read, he would end up passing through, a smile on his lips and a woman at his side. He may want to have sex with her, but he was obviously not losing any sleep over it. In fact, he didn't seem burdened, as she was, with thoughts of the other night. Nor did he alter his unabashed pursuit of pleasure. As he always managed to do, he seemed to have made friends with everyone on board.

The only time she intentionally saw him was during dinner, because they were seated at the same table. She could have eaten the buffet on the Lido deck instead of going to the dining room, but she liked the elegance and didn't want to deny herself the pleasure of experiencing the opulence of the ornate dining room because of Logan. He barely took notice of her anyway. Besides complimenting her on her appearance and politely passing the bread, butter, salt and pepper, he paid her no attention.

They made a couple of more port stops as they slowly traveled down the Argentinean coastline. The weather turned colder and windier. The hot, humid weather of Buenos Aires began to disappear as they traveled out of the heat and into the frosty conditions of the Antarctic. The days also got longer. Sunset moved from eight to nine to ten at night.

Teresa was relieved when the cruise ship approached San Julian. The sooner they arrived, the quicker they'd be able to wrap up this account and go home. Then she could get away from Logan.

She packed her clothes, briefcase, and overnight bag. They still had a two-hour drive to the estancia after disembarking. But the closer they got to port, the more apparent it was they wouldn't be docking. Dark storm clouds settled over the bay, and freezing, thick raindrops pounded the ship. The sea churned wildly, and waves rocked the ship back and forth as if it were nothing but a piece of driftwood. They anchored outside port and the captain announced they would wait for the storm to pass. If they tried to dock, the ship and the pier could be damaged from the massive blows they would sustain from the waves smashing them into each other.

Teresa went to the top-covered deck and stared out at the miserable weather conditions. From the look of the small pier, she was glad the captain decided not to approach. It certainly did seem like a small bump could take it out.

"Looks bad, doesn't it?"

She looked over her shoulder. Logan stood in a wide stance, his arms crossed.

"What will we do if it doesn't get better?" she asked, returning her attention to the storm.

"I guess we wait it out."

Teresa crossed her arms as well and sighed gravely. A profound depression settled in her heart. She thought this idle waiting was almost over. A pleasure cruise where you were all alone was no fun at all.

Logan moved beside her, looking out at the violent ocean. "This is a rough part of Argentina we're going to, Teresa."

"It appears so." She didn't miss the fact he used her real name.

"When we get out there, you follow my lead. Stay close and be cautious."

She lifted her eyes and met his serious gaze. "We're not going to war."

"We don't know what to expect, do we? I don't know what kind of accommodations we'll have. It could be an elaborate estancia or it could be a shack with four walls and a roof."

"You're trying to frighten me."

He reached across and grazed her upper arm. "There's nothing to be afraid of, Tess, I just want us to be careful until we know what we're doing, that's all."

She nodded, finding his strong fingers on her arm thrilling. He must have spent a lot of time in the sun, because he'd bronzed handsomely.

He lowered his hand. "Are you packed?"

"Mm hmm." She nodded again. "I thought we'd be leaving."

"You never did wear those earrings."

She swung her gaze back to his face. He averted his eyes. He sounded hurt, and she felt guilty. He *had* given her a gift after all, and not an inexpensive one. She swallowed her own disappointment. "I'm sorry. Would you like to return them? You still have time."

"I'll tell you what." He faced her with a renewed cheerfulness, full of dogged determination. "We have time to kill. Let's play blackjack. If I win, you wear the earrings tonight. If you win, I take them back."

Teresa wasn't in the mood to play cards, but spending the afternoon with Logan rather than being alone definitely sounded tempting. "Okay, I'll keep score," she said.

He took her hand and led her to the game room. There were board games, dominos, and stacks of cards. Logan took a deck and pointed to the nearest table. "I'm going for a beer. Want one?"

She shrugged. "Sure."

She shuffled the cards and looked outside, wondering how long it would take for the storm to wane.

"Okay, you deal." He slammed the glasses on the table and lifted his leg over the back of the chair as he sat. His posture and rigid facial features suggested he was ready to play a serious game.

She dealt the first hand.

"Hit me," he said.

She dealt him another card. "Damn." He slapped his three cards on the table. He'd gone over twenty-one. She won the hand and noted it on the writing pad.

He took a large gulp of beer. She dealt the second hand. Again, he was too anxious and went over twenty-one. He drank more beer and scowled at her. She reached for her glass, took a sip, and then made another notation on the pad.

On his third hand, he kept the two cards she dealt him, but ended up losing 17 to 20. He took the last few gulps and slammed down his empty glass.

She tried to hold back a smirk, but failed. "Would you like to start on mine?"

"Just deal."

For the next hour, they played in silence, he winning a few hands and she a few. They'd played ruthlessly all the while continuing to have their glasses of beer refilled.

"You're really something, you know that? This is the first time I've had to fight to get a woman to accept a gift."

She glanced at him over her cards. "I felt like you were trying to buy your way into my bed."

He frowned. "Well, you were wrong." He pointed at her hand. "Hit or pass?" It was his turn to deal.

"Hit." She looked at the cards and realized she'd gone over. She handed him her cards.

Rather than taking just the cards, he startled her by grabbing her hand and squeezing her fingers. "I don't buy women. I don't have to."

She held his stare. No, she wouldn't think he'd have to. Logan had a strange kind of sex appeal you didn't even notice at first glance, but then found hard to resist. "Can I have my hand back, please?"

"In a minute." He slid his thumb over the top of her hand tenderly and methodically, all the while studying her.

She lowered her eyes, feeling a flush traveling up her captured arm to her neck and face.

"You're jittery as hell around me. Why?"

She yanked her hand loose. "Don't be ridiculous. Are you dealing or not?"

He placed his elbows on the table and leaned his chin on the back of his hands. "I'm sorry about the other night. I didn't mean to come on so strong, but I thought . . . you know."

She really didn't want to talk about it. Why was he so straightforward about everything? She took a gulp of beer, much like Logan had been doing. "No, I don't know."

"I thought you were just playing hard to get. You seemed turned on."

She finished her glass of beer. Maybe there was something to this gulping down of alcohol. "I was." She signaled for her glass to be refilled. "I wasn't ready to sleep with you, though. Okay? Deal."

They played a few more hands. Logan seemed to drop the subject. He played silently, giving her odd, crooked grins every once in a while.

"What?" she asked.

He shrugged and shook his head.

"Why are you smiling?"

"'Cause I like you, Tess."

She didn't know what to say to that, so she concentrated on her cards. He looked at his cards too, apparently not expecting a reply.

They sat down to play at noon, and by 8:00 pm that night, Teresa was struggling to add up the final score. Her head was swimming. They'd consumed so many glasses of beer that she lost count. They'd talked about everything from Karen's kids to music to politics. Teresa found they had so much in common, she was sorry they hadn't become friends years ago.

"Well, who won?" His voice was hoarse and his eyes bloodshot.

"Dang," she turned the pad of paper over so the numbers were facing the table. "One more hand."

"No, it's dinner time. Who won?"

"Logan, you can return them no matter who won, you know?"

"I won." His lips curled into a smug grin.

"Not by much," she retorted.

"Go upstairs and change. I want to see those earrings hanging against that gorgeous neck of yours."

"Fine." She sighed, "I'll meet you at the dinner table."

She returned to her cabin and pulled out her favorite red dress with the open back. The emerald earrings were beautiful, and Teresa was glad she was wearing them. She was also glad to have spent the day with Logan. Maybe she'd been too rash to reject his proposal so easily without even thinking about it. Maybe he was right. They were together on a luxurious ship. They were attracted to each other, and both were single and available. Would making love to him be such a crazy thing to do? If it were, then perhaps it was time she did something crazy.

CHAPTER TEN

W hen Logan noticed Teresa approaching the dinner table wearing the emeralds, he beamed. "They look great. I knew they would."

He was so proud and looked so wonderful, Teresa couldn't help herself. She leaned into him, her left breast pressing against his arm, and gave him a quick kiss on the lips. "Thank you for the lovely gift," she whispered against his lips.

His smile faded, and his eyes darkened. Without a word, he pulled out a chair for her.

She didn't sit. "I have a confession," she said.

"What?"

"I lied about the card game. You didn't win, I did, but I wanted to keep the emeralds."

He laughed. "I know, I looked at your scorecard. You're a good card player."

"Thanks."

He smiled. "You're good at everything, you know that?"

She touched his chin with her index finger. "Can I have that in writing?"

"Never." He stroked her back, encouraging her to sit. "I'm glad you decided to keep the earrings."

"Me too." She sat, knowing she'd had too much to drink and that she was being deliberately provocative, but she couldn't help herself. "How about some wine?"

"You got it." He ordered a bottle of Chilean Cabernet.

The waiter filled their wine goblets, and she immediately lifted hers, sipped the tangy beverage, and smiled at Logan. When he looked at her with those sexy eyes, she wanted nothing more than to dive into the passion he offered and experience anything and everything that was Logan Wilde.

"Good?" he asked.

She licked her lips. "Delicious."

Logan recognized all the signs. Tonight would be the night. She was ready for him and wouldn't turn him away. But he wasn't so drunk that he didn't know why. She'd sleep with him out of loneliness, but then she'd hate him and herself in the morning. "Kiss me, Tess."

She placed a hand on his knee, brought her lips to his, and offered a wet, erotic kiss that almost knocked him out of his seat. He broke the kiss and winked at her, trying not to react to the heat building in various places within his body. He was right, Tess would never have kissed him like that if she hadn't been drinking beer all day.

"We can skip dinner tonight," she whispered.

None of their table companions had arrived yet. He smiled. As much as he wanted Teresa, and as much as he knew she'd enjoy it, he couldn't go to her room tonight. Not when she'd purposely gotten herself so drunk she could barely walk straight. By the end of their card game, she'd downed her glasses of beer faster than he, and now she was almost finished with her wine.

"Let's get some food in our system, okay?"

"Are you sure?"

He leaned toward her and gave her a quick peck. "I'm positive."

During dinner, he ignored the fact that the waiter had refilled her wine glass several times, but he knew something was up. He flirted back as aggressively as she did, had a good time, but stopped drinking himself. At the end of the meal, he walked her out of the dining room.

"Can you make it back to your stateroom alone?" he asked.

She gave him a sexy smile and took his hand. "I don't think I want to try."

He put his arm around her waist and nibbled on her neck. They were standing in the dining room lobby, acting completely inappropriate, but he didn't care, and she didn't know what she was doing.

"Tess, you look damn sexy tonight, you know that?"

She wrapped her arms around his shoulder. "Does that mean you still want me?"

He groaned. "Yeah, I want you, you know that."

"Take me to my cabin, Logan."

Okay, he'd take her, but then he'd leave. He wouldn't sleep with her. He wouldn't take advantage of her while she was like this.

But when they opened the door to her cabin, she pulled him inside and began kissing him with an intensity he'd only fantasized about. He walked her backwards until she collapsed on the bed. He'd lie beside her, but only for a second—he wouldn't stay.

Her fingers danced along his chest, undoing buttons with the ease of a woman with a mission. And he was her mission, her goal. Lord, he was excited! When her hands moved to his pants, he stopped her, pulling her hands above her head. "What's your hurry? You're still fully dressed."

"That's because you haven't taken any of my clothes off yet."

Logan closed his eyes and swallowed. He could do this. "I'm not going to, Tess." His voice sounded strained, but he'd said it.

"You want to watch while I take them off?"

His erection just hit tilt. He wanted her so bad, it hurt. He wanted to scream, "Yes, take it all off!" but it wasn't fair, he kept repeating to himself. "You had too much to drink, honey."

"I'm kind of buzzed, but I know what I'm doing."

"Do you?"

"Yes, now let go of my hands so I can free you."

"Damn." He let go of her hands, but jumped off her bed. "I can't take any more. I've gotta go." He buttoned his shirt hastily.

She sat. "Logan? What's wrong?"

"Don't you know what I want to do to you?" She looked rumpled and sexy and so damn willing.

"Yes, I do. It's okay, I want you to."

"No, you don't." He eyed her suspiciously.

Her brows furrowed. "I don't?"

He shook his head. "You're drunk, Tess."

She lowered her head as if overcome with shame. "But I'd want you even if I wasn't drunk," she said without looking at him.

"Great, sober up, then come and see me. You know where my room is."

"Don't leave, Logan. Please." Her eyes were shiny with tears. "The alcohol is giving me more courage, but I know what I want. You said no strings, no commitments, just sex, just fun. That's what I want."

"What about tomorrow morning when you realize what you did and you decide you want to kill me?"

"I won't. I promise." She stood and walked up to him.

She did look like she knew what she wanted, but how could she when she couldn't even walk straight? He curled his index finger under her chin to lift her face and ran his thumb across her sexy, red lips. "Why tonight, Tess? A few nights ago, you threw me out."

She stared at him long and hard, and he wondered if she was going to answer. "I changed my mind. I want you to hold me close tonight. I want to feel your lips on mine, on my breasts. I want your hands to touch me all over, and I want to know what it feels like to have your body pressed against mine as you move inside me. I've . . . I've never felt that before."

Logan stood stunned. "You mean never with me?"

She placed her hand over his and took it away from her face. "I mean never."

He inhaled sharply and took a step back, pulling his hand out of hers. "Oh—my—God. Are you trying to tell me you're a virgin?"

She frowned. "Yes, but—"

"Yes! Yes, you're a virgin?" He ran his fingers through his hair, trying to think straight. This wasn't what he was looking for at all. The last time he'd slept with a virgin, he'd been eighteen years old. He fixed a steady look on her. She looked hurt and confused. He sighed. He couldn't just walk away now.

Logan encircled her waist and pulled her against him. "Look, Tess, I don't know what's going through your mind right now, but the first time should be special, and it shouldn't be while you're drunk, with someone like me."

"Then make it special for me."

Oh man. He lowered his head, his forehead resting on top of her head. He caressed her back, feeling a strange tenderness he'd never felt for any woman before. "I'll tell you what—if you still feel this way come morning, then maybe."

She gazed up at him, then tilted her face and stretched to kiss him. He tasted her lips, but held back. "Tess, I really want you and I really like you, but this isn't going to happen tonight, okay?"

"But, Logan—"

"I mean it, Tess."

She lowered her gaze, then moved out his arms unsteadily. "Can you go now?"

He buried his hands in his pockets so he wouldn't be tempted to touch her again. "Yeah." He walked backwards, watching as she sat miserably on her bed. "You okay?"

She nodded, but she didn't look up at him.

"You'll thank me come morning."

She nodded again. "Please leave."

Logan turned around and left, cursing her in a million different ways under his breath. Why didn't she tell him from the very beginning? He wouldn't have bothered getting wound up over her. Then he almost laughed out loud. *Admit it, you never had any control over what you felt for her. Never.*

CHAPTER ELEVEN

How do you face a man after you offered yourself to him like a piece of meat and he rejected you? Teresa sat miserably in the Lido cafe, downing liters of coffee. She only slept a couple of hours last night after he left, and when she awoke, her head felt like there was a base drum inside, keeping beat with her heart.

Whoever said being a virgin was good? Logan cleared away from her like she had the plague. At twenty-eight, being a virgin was weird; at least that was the way men made her feel. She shouldn't have told him.

"There you are. I waited for you at breakfast."

She forced her head up and looked across the table where Logan was making himself comfortable. Why was he yelling at her? "I couldn't eat breakfast."

"You okay?"

"Shhh, not so loud."

He chuckled. "We've docked. It's time to disembark. Are you ready to go?"

She nodded, holding her temples with her fingertips. If she didn't, she was sure her head would split apart.

"Actually, you should eat. Let me get you some toast or something."

Before she could say no, he was gone. He brought her a toasted bagel with cream cheese. It looked repulsive, but she took it anyway and began to eat.

He watched her so intently, she began to feel self-conscious. "Why don't you go do something?"

"I have nothing to do."

"Stop staring at me."

"You're beautiful—"

"Don't. Nothing you can say will make me feel better, so don't even try."

He smiled. "Hey, I was hoping you'd be able to make *me* feel better. Tell me I wasn't a fool for leaving last night."

"You were a perfect gentleman. Congratulations."

He laughed. "Thank you."

She leveled him as serious a stare as she could muster. "You didn't have to leave. I knew what I was doing."

He planted his forearms on the table and leaned forward. "Lady, you didn't want to make love to me. If you did, you wouldn't have tried to numb yourself with gallons of alcohol."

"I didn't—"

"Bull."

"Okay, maybe I did. I was a little nervous."

"Tess, you're a smart woman. Figure out what you want and go for it, sober and consciously. See you downstairs."

***

Logan grabbed Teresa's hand as they walked down the gangway. She insisted on carrying her own bag, but he at least wanted to hold on to her. "There's a pickup, Tess. Think that's our ride?"

"I'll ask."

She handed him her bag and darted around the other tourists who stood looking at the small port of San Julian. Most people were taking a tourist bus on a three-hour drive to see *Perito Moreno*, the largest moving glacier on land. The port was used mostly to transport wool or fish. The air was so cold and crisp he could see his breath. Logan kept an eye on Teresa, following closely behind her.

She spoke in rapid Spanish to the bored-looking man who leaned on his olive green 1955 Ford pickup. Rather than looking her in the eyes as she spoke, he swept his gaze arrogantly down her body. Typical male behavior meant to put women in their place, intimidate them, make them uncomfortable.

Logan's anger rose uncharacteristically fast. He was just about to step forward and tell that dirty pig to keep his eyes, thoughts, and everything else off Teresa when she fired off some more Spanish. This time, however, it was delivered in a harsh, loud voice, which made the man stand upright. He opened his mouth to say something, but Teresa continued the tirade, so he nodded, glanced at Logan, and moved behind the steering wheel. She threw a look over her shoulder at Logan and smiled. "This is it."

"What's wrong?" Logan asked, eyeing the guy in the truck.

"Nothing."

Logan opened the door, and she made a move to get in, but he wasn't about to let her sit next to the slob. He took her elbow. "I'll go first."

She didn't argue, letting Logan sit in the middle. The man didn't say a word the entire two-hour drive down the dusty gravel road.

Teresa drank lots of bottled water and swallowed painkillers for her headache.

The land was cold and had the appearance of a desert. Small brush-like chaparral covered the terrain, bouncing along with the wind, which blew constantly. Since it had rained, there was no dust, but it was obvious that the wind normally would be accompanied by dirt.

El Gaucho Estancia came into view as soon as they turned left onto a smaller dirt road. Thousands of sheep surrounded the land. The estancia wasn't as bad as Logan had expected. The driver stopped the pickup in front of an extended white building with large windows.

"*Vamos,*" he said.

"Let's go, Logan, he's taking us inside."

"What about our bags?"

"They will be taken to you," the man said in poorly pronounced English.

Logan and Teresa glanced at each other and shrugged.

"Welcome, welcome." A thin man with white hair and a mustache came forward and shook his hand. He smiled at Teresa and kissed both her cheeks.

Logan tensed.

"I am called Senor Manuel Pennetti. You have been stuck in a bad storm."

"Yes," Logan nodded.

"I know you are tired, yes? Well,"—he clapped his hands togeth-er—"I have your guest rooms ready."

They were given adjoining rooms, and Logan noticed Teresa's quick glance his way. No doubt, she was thinking about last night. It cracked him up that she was so embarrassed. But in truth, sleeping so close to her would be difficult. Just because he knew he couldn't have her, didn't make him stop wanting her. He had no right to expect Tess to allow him into her bed, but now that he knew she was interested, he expected it to happen. Although he knew it would be wrong, that it would be her first time, and that she might attach special significance to their union, he still wanted her. But now, they were officially working together, and he had to concentrate on what they'd come here to do.

"Tonight, we can meet with my family, after you rest, yes?"

"That's very kind of you, thank you," Tess said.

"You will eat dinner with me in about four hours?" He phrased it as a question, but it was meant as a directive.

Their bags were brought up and they were left to move into their rooms. In the dimly lit hallway, Logan noticed how Teresa hesitated before she lifted her bag over her shoulder and eased toward her room.

"Want me to help you with anything?"

Her eyes lifted, and she gave him an almost shy look. "No, I'm fine. guess, after dinner we can go over our plan for tomorrow."

Logan wanted to touch her, kiss her the way he had yesterday. What was wrong with him? Why did he have this need to hold her and reassure both her and himself that everything was okay between them? "Good idea, Tess, but don't get overly eager, okay? I want them to show us around. We need to see the product, their operation. They need to sell this place to us, not the other way around. We shouldn't appear too interested."

She lifted an eyebrow. "Is that your plan?"

He shrugged. "It's a strategy that works well. If they think they want us more than we want them, we'll get a better deal when we do negotiate."

She watched him with a pensive look on her face. "All right, we let them sell it."

***

Teresa was still tired after her three-hour nap, but her body appreciated being on solid ground again, and her head had stopped pounding. After a long, warm shower, her skin tingled and felt velvety soft from the moisturizing bath gel she generously lathered over her salt-air-exposed body. She bunched her hair up on her head and chose a simple, flowing, white cotton dress and sandals for dinner, hoping Senor Pennetti wasn't having a formal meal.

Teresa was pleased when Pennetti ushered both her and Logan onto a flower-covered veranda. His family included his mother and two sons, one which was their moody driver from this afternoon, except now he was clean. Pennetti explained that his wife spent most of the time running the business offices in Buenos Aires, not a fan of their lifestyle in Patagonia. They all shook hands.

Logan dressed casually in snug, faded jeans that rode low on his hips and a tan golf shirt. His hair was damp and combed back, his face clean-shaven. He sat beside Teresa, looking as tired as she. He'd been more distant since yesterday, which made Teresa unhappy. Now that she'd begun to feel closer to him, she didn't want him to withdraw.

Luckily, a light meal of *empanadas*—small meat pies—was served along with paper-thin sandwiches, pickled vegetables, and wine. They didn't speak business at all; instead, Senor Pennetti kept the conversation casual and spoke to them as he would have with friends.

"I hope this is enough food. I did not think you would want a big meal."

"This is perfect," Teresa reassured him. Logan echoed her words.

"I have eaten Mexican food, Ms. Romero, and it is very spicy." Pennetti smiled.

She smiled back and nodded. "It can be."

"Teresa's parents own a Mexican restaurant in California," Logan shared.

Senor Pennetti raised an eyebrow. "Is that right?"

She glanced at Logan, then back at Pennetti. "Yes. They opened it years ago when my sister and I were little girls. We used to help set the tables and put up decorations. It's loved by the community and always filled with locals."

Pennetti nodded, a warm smile on his lips. He shifted his eyes to Logan. "And your parents?"

Logan had been watching Teresa strangely, but at the question of his parents, he sighed and turned his attention to Manuel Pennetti. "My father was an accountant, and my mother worked part-time as a store clerk. They died while I was still quite young."

"A shame," Pennetti said.

Logan shrugged. "Your sons work with you, huh?"

Senor Pennetti waved a hand across the table at the two young men sitting politely as their father spoke. "I could not get by without them. They are young and strong and do things I get too tired to do anymore. Their English is poor, though."

"Juan Carlos," Logan said, pointing to their afternoon driver, "speaks English fine."

Manuel Pennetti eyed his son. "Juan Carlos does not accept that we live in a global economy yet, but is beginning to understand."

Teresa didn't think he accepted or understood, and by the way Logan was staring at the young man, she guessed he didn't think so either. Juan Carlos was not openly hostile, probably out of respect for his father, but Teresa had no doubt he didn't want them there.

After exchanging a few more pleasantries, they agreed to meet early the next morning for a tour of the estancia. Logan climbed the stairs beside her, and she was sharply aware of his every move. When he touched her upper arm, she nearly missed the top step.

"You look sweet and feminine tonight, Tess."

She smiled. "I wasn't in the mood for a business suit tonight."

"Thank God."

"Did you want to go over anything tonight, or do you want to wait to see the operation tomorrow first?"

He seemed to force himself to pry his gaze off her dress and meet her eyes. "Ah . . . well, I'm, ah, a little tired."

"We'll talk tomorrow then. I'd like to turn in too."

He nodded. "Okay."

She looked down, not knowing what else to say, but not wanting to go into her bedroom alone. "Good night."

He looked at her lips, then her eyes. "Hey Tess, why do you look sad when you talk about your parents' restaurant?"

Stunned by his question, she asked. "Do I?"

"Yep. You looked sad when Carla was telling me about it, and you looked sad tonight when you were talking about it yourself."

She looked over his shoulder at a white wall. She hadn't realized she was that expressive. "I love that place. My parents used to say it gave them freedom. They raised us on what they made from that restaurant." She sighed and looked into Logan's eyes. "They've borrowed money against the restaurant to pay for some unexpected things. My mom had a couple of operations . . . ."

He stepped closer to her and angled his head. His deep brown eyes seemed to soak in her soul. "And now they've got to pay back the debts."

She nodded. "I just don't ever want to see them lose the restaurant that's so much a part of who they are. They brought a little piece of Mexico with them when they came to California, and it's right there in the restaurant."

Logan caressed her cheek with the back of his hand as he'd done that night on her porch. "And it's part of you," he whispered.

She was drawn to his eyes as if they were magnets. She couldn't look away. She wanted him to kiss her more than anything in the world. If he'd wrap his arms around her and share one of his overpowering yet giving kisses with her, she'd feel so much better. She leaned her face against the back of his hand. *Kiss me, please kiss me.*

"Everything will work out, Tess. Don't worry," he said and eased away from her, breaking the enchanting spell she'd gladly stay under forever.

She nodded, unable to speak.

He took her hand, opened her bedroom door, and winked. "You'll have to do the rest yourself."

She smiled. "Sleep well." Then she slipped inside before she did something stupid like ask him to come in with her.

She scanned the empty room and sighed. The best thing for her to do was to climb into bed and go to sleep to make sure she was alert and effective tomorrow morning.

The knock on her door startled her as she was kicking off her sandals and taking the pin out of her bun to let her hair fall loose. Did Logan change his mind about working tonight?

"Come in," she called.

The door opened, and Juan Carlos stood glaring at her. "I'd like to talk to you," he said in Spanish.

Teresa nodded. "Come in."

When he walked in and shut the door behind him, Teresa wondered if inviting him into her bedroom was such a good idea.

He shoved his hands in his pockets. "I have no interest in doing business with a foreign company," he said, not wasting time with small talk.

Teresa already figured that out. She nodded. I can understand why you'd have reservations."

"No." He smiled coldly. "I said I do not want to do business with you. I am certain. I have no reservations."

"Your father obviously disagrees with—"

"My father is falling for the same tricks the majority of the businesses in Argentina are. Our country is being bought out by foreigners. We've sold our railroads, our telephones, our airplanes. We have nothing of our own left. I won't see our farm sold out that way."

Teresa frowned as she looked at his angry face. "We're not buying your farm. We want to buy your products. You're in business to sell wool. We want to buy. That's all."

He stepped closer. "Teresa, you're Latina. That's why I came to you, figuring you'd understand."

"I'm a buyer, a business person, not a politician."

He gave her a disgusted look. "You're a sellout," he said and left before she could answer.

She slumped onto her bed and sighed. Great, another problem.

CHAPTER
TWELVE

The next morning, they walked to the shearing barn across the field from the main house. Señor Pennetti was a friendly man. He treated Teresa and Logan as true guests, making them feel comfortable.

Logan began to think the negotiations would go easier than he'd feared. Señor Pennetti was obviously pleased to have them there. He pointed out parcels of land and explained that the arid conditions didn't allow them to grow many crops. His permanent ranch hands tended to the sheep and maintained the buildings during the off-season. The nomadic workers came for the season, and the sheep shearing began.

Pennetti came to a halt, switched to Spanish, and placed a hand on Teresa's shoulder as he spoke.

Logan watched her backside clad in form-fitting black pants as she walked. He moved beside her. "What's he saying?"

Teresa put up a hand to silence Logan and continued to listen to Pennetti. For some reason, he felt annoyed, not so much because he didn't understand a damn thing they were saying, but because she was practically ignoring him.

He exhaled heavily and began walking toward the enormous shed-looking building. Inside, he found an almost festive atmosphere. Loud Spanish music seemed to motivate the workers as they held a sheep between their legs and ran the shears down the side of its body, leaving neat little rows of short fleece. When the men finished with four or five sheep, they wiped their sweaty bodies with a rag and drank something that looked like wine.

"My men can shear one hundred sheep a day, sometimes one hundred ten," Pennetti explained.

Logan hadn't realized Pennetti and Tess were standing behind him. "Each man?" he asked without turning around.

"Of course," Pennetti's proud voice was loud, rising above the sound of the shearing and talking men.

Logan had done his research, no matter what Teresa thought, and he knew this was the most productive estancia in the country. "You don't seem to have many men, though."

"I can if I need to." He stood beside Logan now. "Only about a third of my stock is in use."

He decided to give the man something to worry about. "If we were to contract with you, we'd need the other two-thirds sheared this year."

Pennetti moved closer to Logan, his hands flying as he spoke. "Shearing season is close to an end. I have sent workers away. For next year, yes?"

Logan shook his head in an unhurried manner. "You forget, Mr. Pennetti, your summer is our winter. It took you most of the season just to agree to see us. Winter in America is almost over, so what we purchase this year *is* for next year."

Teresa was frowning almost as much as Pennetti was, but Pennetti was concentrating too intensely on Logan to notice. She had to know Logan was bluffing. Purchases were always made a year in advance. The wool purchased this year would be processed and woven for the following winter. He leveled a look at her, hoping she'd understand. She did. Her expression changed, and she smiled at Pennetti, touching his shoulder. Pennetti turned a half-worried, half-angry expression toward her.

"Señor Pennetti," she began. "We don't mean to upset you, but we chose you because of your reputation. If need be, perhaps you can manage to solicit more help and get the rest of your stock prepared."

His expression softened. "Señorita, it was my understanding you were going to look at my business and we were going to contract for next year." He spoke in a sing-song manner that pleaded for her understanding.

"That gives us a year to shop around then." Logan was firm, but not rude or confrontational.

Pennetti's arms went out in resignation. "Yes, of course, if it is what you want."

"If you meet our needs, we want you," Teresa said.

Logan cursed inwardly. Didn't he tell her not to appear too damn eager? He felt like pulling her aside and sticking masking tape on her mouth.

"Let's go with that, then," Logan addressed Pennetti. "Let's see if you do meet our needs, or the point is mute, isn't that right, Ms. Romero?"

She glanced at him and nodded. "Right."

Pennetti walked them through the shearing facility, where Logan and Teresa were able to inspect the wool preparation. The shearers carefully sorted different quality wool, discarding contaminated, stained, or colored fibers.

"Do you ensure quality control through your sorting and packaging methods?" Logan asked.

Manuel Pennetti nodded. "We sort sheep before shearing and package wool separately. Come, I will show you."

Teresa followed silently.

Pennetti pointed to a slatted table where workers were combing through fleece already sheared, further searching out inferior wool. They were quick and thorough. Logan eyed Teresa while she watched the workers with rapt attention. He loved watching her at work. She always appeared to be genuinely interested in the project at hand.

"You will be wanting the white, finer wool, yes?"

"Yes." Teresa said.

Pennetti smiled. He took her hand and placed a handful of woolen fibers in her palm. "Notice the length of these fibers, short, perfect for fine sweaters. Why, these are so perfect they can even be spun for suits."

Logan admired the fibers over her shoulder while she separated them with her fingers. They certainly were good quality. Pennetti was bragging and selling his product just like Logan wanted, and that pleased him. But the wool didn't hold his attention long. Standing behind Teresa and watching her long, delicate fingers play with the soft white threads distracted him. Two fingers of each hand had rings. Her fingernails were not too long, but perfectly manicured and painted in a reddish color.

He glanced at her neck and had to fight the urge to kiss it.

"Do you see Mr. Wilde?"

Logan glanced at Pennetti. "Impressive," he said.

"You will not easily find this kind of quality."

He couldn't help but look at Teresa again. "You might be right."

She turned then and held out her hand. "Sorry, would you like to inspect the fibers?"

He took the wool and fingered the fibers as she had. Then returned them to Pennetti without a word.

They finished the tour through the facility, then climbed into a faded, old army jeep with chipped paint on the doors and sides. They rode around the site, learning about the layout. Logan noted how Pennetti offered her the seat beside him and relegated Logan to the back.

The topography of the land was excellent for drainage. It provided sufficient shelter and shade for the animals. They had access to water, and the shearing buildings had electricity. Logan was pleased. This site seemed to be as impressive as he'd read about and knew Edward would tell him to secure the account.

As they returned to the estancia, he addressed Pennetti. "You have a large operation. Do you think you could supply what we need?"

"Of course I'd like to see your requirements Mr. Wilde, but I think we can."

"I'd like to see a Micron Test Report on the flocks."

"Sure."

"And your management schedule. I want to know how you clean your facilities, feeding practices, pasture management, everything and anything that can affect wool quality."

Pennetti frowned. "It is your right. I will supply all that information."

"When you do, we can talk further. And see what you can do about having the rest of the flocks sheared this year."

Pennetti gave a short stiff nod and headed for the ranch house.

***

"Are you trying to lose the account?" Teresa asked as soon as Pennetti was out of earshot. She turned on her usual austere office personality, only it seemed angrier when directed at him.

The wind blew incessantly, little dirt devils twirled around, and Logan sat on a log, staring at the landscape.

"Well?" She stood in front of him.

He let his gaze travel up her body and found himself getting aroused. Many times today, he'd thought of where they'd left off on the ship. How he'd like to go upstairs and climb into bed with her and forget any talk of work. "Why would I be trying to do that?" He squinted one eye and looked at her face.

"It's not smart to antagonize the client the first day out."

"I thought I explained my strategy to you."

"There's no need to be that aggressive and bait the man. He was being very kind."

Logan leaned back on the log. "Don't question my methods, Tess, and don't interrupt me again when I'm engaged in a business dealing. You almost blew it in that shearing barn."

She opened her mouth, gaping down at him, a lovely flush appearing on her cheeks. "This is *our* account, and if you're mishandling it, you bet I'm going to interrupt."

Logan stood, deciding it was better to be at eye level with her. "You're out of your league here, Tess. Just keep your mouth shut and learn how this is done."

Her eyes narrowed, and he knew that, unfortunately, he was provoking her, but even though he didn't want to fight, he was going to handle this account his way.

"The only thing I'll learn from you is how to be rude and unreasonable. I'm going to go apologize to Pennetti and make sure he understands we have no intention of going elsewhere."

Logan restrained her arm. "No, you're not going to do that." He didn't raise his voice above normal, but he kept a steady gaze on her so she'd know he meant business.

"Let me go, Logan." Her voice was low and shaky. She was furious with him, and he knew it.

He pulled her closer. "I know what I'm doing." He spoke close to her ear.

Teresa stiffened. He was too close, solid and unyielding. Through her peripheral vision, she caught sight of his long, masculine neck. She felt her anger begin to transform into yearning, and a shiver spirited through her body. "And what's that?" Her throat was dry.

Logan always looked cool, almost dispassionate. He moved his hand from her upper arm toward her shoulder. She'd already realized he was a tactile man and his touches didn't mean anything, but Teresa couldn't help the tightness in her stomach anytime his hand was on or near her body.

"We put him on the defensive. He proves to us he's worthy."

"I won't create an antagonistic work relationship with Pennetti. I don't work like that."

He smiled. "What do you do? Become his best friend? I saw the way he watched your tight ass in those pants. Is that your strategy, show off the goods until he buys? You know, I was only kidding when I suggested that on the ship."

He delivered those words cleanly and maliciously, and they stung worse than a slap on the face. Teresa's fury came rushing back. What was she supposed to wear on a tour of a sheep farm? She pulled her shoulder free of his tight grip. "You're a pig, Logan."

"I'm not the one flaunting the body and flirting, sweetheart."

Her face was on fire. She'd never had an urge to slap someone as much as she did right now. She made a 180-degree turn and began walking away from him before she said or did something she couldn't take back. Besides, she felt the sting of tears behind her eyes, and crying was unacceptable.

"Tess, come back here." Logan's voice sounded resigned. "Tess." A little louder. "Damn it, Tess."

She didn't stop.

"I'm right. I've been at this business twice as long as you have." He was shouting now.

She continued to walk.

"You're so damn stubborn, and you won't listen to reason. Stop, or I'll call Edward. I won't work with you like this."

She stopped and turned to look at him. "Like what?"

They were about twenty yards apart.

"You're acting like . . . like . . . like a woman."

"Like a woman? As opposed to like a man?"

"You know what I mean. You're throwing a little-girl fit and walking away instead of debating with me as a business partner."

It was all she could do to keep from screaming at the top of her lungs. "Debating? Is that what you call this?" She shook her head. "You're the one who resorted to personal attacks. If you think I'm going to stand around and allow you to hurl degrading insults at me because we shared a kiss, forget it."

He laughed with a definite lack of amusement in his voice. "And if you were hoping I'd turn over control just because you were willing to turn over your body, *you're* wrong."

What? Where did that come from? He was being deliberately cruel, and she couldn't figure out why. He had to know his words would hurt her, yet he didn't seem to care. If there was one thing she didn't think Logan was, was cruel. She never thought he'd use the personal, private moment they shared against her in business. She swallowed her tears and forced herself to respond. "I can't take back what happened between us, I'm not even sure I'd want to, but I can promise it'll never happen again—"

"Tess—"

"I don't want to control you or this account. But I won't shut up and listen to you treat a client disrespectfully. You either work with me and we agree on the strategy ahead of time, or don't expect any support from me."

"I thought we had agreed."

She turned around and continued toward the estancia.

"We talked about it last night, Tess. You agreed not to act too interested, and you were kissing Pennetti's ass." He was on her heels now. Before she reached the door, he ran in front of her and stopped dead. She tried to go around him, but he blocked her way.

"I *will* call Edward, and you'll be gone, Tess."

"Think so?"

"I know it."

"You don't know anything. You can't pull this off without me, and that's a fact. And just to set the record straight, I wasn't kissing Pennetti's ass, and I wasn't flirting with him. I was being friendly. Haven't you noticed how much slower the pace is here? How warm and social people are?"

"We're not here to be friends. We're here on business."

She shook her head. "You're approaching this all wrong because you don't understand the culture, and you're so self-centered, you don't even see it."

He narrowed his eyes. "I knew you were trouble. You were the last person I wanted to work with."

Teresa swallowed the hurt. She saw the truth in his eyes. "I know it. You haven't worked with me yet, Wilde, not one day."

"I've tried."

She shook her head. "You lied when you came into my office and said we could do this together. You meant we could do it your way."

The creases on his forehead eased. His whole face calmed. "I didn't lie. You tried to, I mean . . . damn. You're right, I give up, I can't do this."

He disappeared inside the house. Teresa watched him leave, lowered her head, and turned back toward the empty land. She began walking, not knowing where she was going, but she no longer felt like going to her room.

She'd been depressed enough during the tour when she heard Logan asking all those wonderful questions that never occurred to her. She'd thought she was the one who was most prepared, but in reality, it seemed he was. He was right; she was too intent on getting the client and didn't concentrate enough on making sure the client was worth acquiring. She still had a lot to learn, but to have Logan remind her of that and tell her to shut up and listen was just too much.

More humiliating still was that he thought she'd agreed to sleep with him to manipulate him in business. How little he thought of her and of her desire to make love to him. She thought it would be special, beautiful, for both of them, but apparently, she was wrong.

"Where do you think you're going?"

She'd been in such deep thought, she hadn't even heard Juan Carlos gallop up beside her. "Just walking," she said.

He jumped off his horse and fell into step beside her. "The wind is picking up. It's not safe to go far."

She gazed at him. The last thing she wanted was another man telling her what to do. "Don't worry about this '*sell-out*'—I'll be fine."

He smiled. "Ms. Romero. I must insist."

She ignored him and continued to walk. She just wanted to be left alone.

"Teresa," he switched to Spanish. "I have one free hour. Tell me about your company, and if you can convince me I should do business with you in that time, you'll have a wool supplier. If not, I will talk to my father, and I promise you, our business will be over."

Teresa stopped walking and stared at this arrogant young man. He had to be in his very early twenties, and although she didn't believe he could sway his father's decision as much as he claimed, one thing was true: Juan Carlos and his brother were the future owners of *El Gaucho Estancia*.

"You know deep inside that there are countless benefits for your farm if we were to take you on, but if you want me to spell it all out for you, okay."

He waved an arm back toward the estancia and shearing barn. "After you."

CHAPTER THIRTEEN

Logan sat against the headboard of his bed. The clock on the nightstand indicated it was 10:00 pm. Outside, enough daylight remained to actually allow people to work. Music and voices continued to filter up to his room from the sheep shearing barn. His window was open just enough to let some night air blow in, but with it he smelled the unmistakable aroma of barbecued beef. The previous night, they'd also eaten between 10:00 pm and 11:00 pm. Logan's belly grumbled, he wasn't used to eating so late.

He flung himself off the bed and walked out to the hallway to knock on Teresa's door.

"Tess, open up."

Silence was his only reply.

"We'll have to go eat in a bit."

There was absolutely no sound coming from her bedroom. No matter what, they had to appear united in front of their client. He'd been feeling like a jerk the past few hours for upsetting her. He didn't like to argue because it solved nothing. Life was better when you kept your cool and went through the day calm and mellow. Unfortunately, Teresa evoked too many feelings he was used to keeping in check. He'd lashed out at her, purposely wanting to bring her down a couple of notches, but his mouth had spewed out ugly venom before he could stop himself.

Now she was angry, maybe hurt, he was miserable, and all this was definitely bad for business. He refused to fight with her anymore. Time to apologize. Logan lifted the European handle and slowly opened her bedroom door. "Tess?"

He looked around and verified it was indeed empty. Where the hell was she?

He left his room and checked the obvious places: kitchen, living room, library. The public rooms were empty. Maybe she went for a walk outside. He took a lap around the large, brick house and didn't see her. Logan placed his hands on his hips and glanced at the barn. She couldn't be in there, could she? He saw Juan Carlos strolling back from the barn. Logan crossed the dusty, wind-blown field and met Juan Carlos halfway. The music got louder as he approached.

"You're looking for your sexy coworker?"

Logan narrowed his eyes. "Is she in there?"

"Yes, I'm finished with her. My men are enjoying her now."

Logan's heart dropped to his stomach. His whole body tightened. He was going to tear this cocky Argentine to shreds. No, he was going to hang himself if anything happened to Tess. He had no business leaving her alone. He'd let a stupid argument and his pride cloud his thinking. "Get the hell out of my way." He pushed Juan Carlos aside and hurried to the barn.

When he reached the garage-sized sliding door, he slipped inside and was stunned and relieved by what he saw. At one end of the barn, men had a huge grill where at least half a cow seemed to be spread out, complete with sausages and various types of internal organs. His stomach lurched at the sight. The men drank wine from the bottle as they waited for their dinner, talking loudly, laughing, and singing along to the music, with Teresa at the center of attention, still dressed in her skin-tight black pants and body-hugging, black, stretch top.

About twenty men stood beside her or sat on wooden railings in rapt attention as she spoke in rapid Spanish. Logan's faded anger revived again. What in the world was she doing? The woman was crazy. It occurred to him that his anger had nothing to do with her jeopardizing the account but more with the attention she was receiving from so many men. He was jealous.

Logan continued to move forward until someone noticed and pointed at him, saying God knows what.

Teresa's head snapped back. She met his eyes. They stared at each other for a few seconds, then she stood and strolled toward him. "Come in."

Don't blow it. Keep calm. He didn't want to make a fool of himself. Besides, he had no right to be jealous, and he was glad she was okay. "What are you doing?"

"Just hanging out, waiting for dinner. Come meet the guys."

He wanted to drag her out or at least throw a heavy blanket around her, but he nodded. "All right." At least if she was still upset with him, she was concealing it for the benefit of others. He could do the same.

"This is Pablo, he's like the foreman. Raul, Miguel..." She continued down the line, naming every guy in the barn. How she remembered all the names was a mystery.

"This is my partner, Logan."

They all said hello.

"They were telling me a little about the operation. They've got some funny stories."

Logan smiled at her, though that was the last thing he felt like doing. "And what were you telling them that kept them so enthralled?"

"Oh, they wanted to know about the U.S., what we eat, how we live, they're very interested."

I bet. They're interested in anything you have to say as long as they can continue to look at you.

Logan leaned against a wooden railing and folded his arms across his chest. He couldn't help but glance at the way the material of her shirt stretched smoothly over her breasts. Damn, but she looked good. "Sounds like you've been having a good time."

She didn't answer him. But she didn't have to; the derisive look she gave him said it all. She sat back in the only decent chair in the place and continued to talk animatedly. Logan watched and listened, though he didn't understand a thing. She translated every once in a while when she felt he needed to know what they were saying.

The longer he watched her, the better she looked to him, and the greater was the tenderness he felt inside for her. He also realized that the men weren't leering but listened with real interest. Although they were undeniably smitten, they were respectful, and their eyes shone with admiration for this American woman who treated them with kindness and importance.

When the meat was cooked, they passed out wooden boards and slapped portions of short ribs on them. Everyone ate and talked happily as if they were all part of a large extended family. Boy, could these people talk. Logan enjoyed himself despite his lack of understanding. The beef was the juiciest, tastiest he'd ever had. By one in the morning, they were finally finished eating and partying.

"We'd better turn in." He took Teresa's arm.

She'd eaten a full meal for the first time since they started this trip. Logan didn't think she was capable of eating as much as she had. With her food, she consumed an entire bottle of red wine, but that didn't surprise him. He knew she could drink.

"They say they're going to play cards now. Are you sure you don't want to stay?"

Logan shook his head. "No, it's late."

"I'll stay," she announced happily. "I can learn another game."

Oh no, she wasn't staying. He smiled at her. "It's late, Tess. It's time for us to go to bed."

Her eyes widened. "Bed? Is that an invitation?"

That wasn't what he'd meant. "Would you like it to be?"

She blushed. "I'm not drunk enough to agree to sleep with you this time, Logan. And if you think you're forgiven for what you said this afternoon, forget it."

"I was wrong." He was, and he meant it.

"And?"

"And that's it. I shouldn't have said the things I said."

She narrowed her eyes. "I'm still not sleeping with you."

He laughed and let her arm go. "Well, I wasn't inviting you to, but you will. Someday."

Her eyes remained hooded, and the corner of her lips lifted into a sexy smile he had a hard time resisting.

"*Juegan*?" The men asked, interrupting.

"Won't you, Tess?"

"I got the feeling you were no longer interested in doing anything with me," her voice was soft, lamenting.

"Teresa," Pablo called her again since she'd either ignored or not heard his last invitation to play.

She shook her head. "*No, Pablo, gracias.*" She faced Logan again. "Let's go."

He followed her out. A cool, strong wind howled outside. They walked alongside the barn wall for protection. She stopped suddenly and gazed at him. "I feel like a fool for what happened between us on that ship, Logan."

He reached for her, but she stepped back. "No, don't. I threw myself at you like . . . like the women you probably pick up in bars and—"

"You were drunk."

"Stop saying that. I knew exactly what I was doing. There's no excuse for what I did. I was wrong."

"Hey, did you forget it was *me* who was pursuing *you*?"

She bit her bottom lip with her top lip and shook her head. "It's complicated things between us and—"

"It has not, Tess, I—"

"It has! I'm feeling hurt because of what you said to me this afternoon. I'm angry with you, yet I want you to hold me. I'm all mixed up."

This time when he reached across, he gripped her shoulders and pulled her against him. "You're feeling hurt because I acted like a jerk. I was pissed at you, so I said things I knew would hurt you."

Her tear-filled eyes shifted off his face.

He swallowed to open his quickly closing throat. He'd never seen Tess like this before. She wasn't the crybaby type. He leaned his forehead against hers and closed his eyes. "Oh, Tess. I'm sorry."

"Me too."

"Are you sorry you wanted me? Please don't be sorry about that."

She shook her head against his, then eased back and looked into his eyes. "I told you this afternoon, I'm not sorry about that." She gave a short hiccuppy laugh. "Humiliated, yes. Sorry, no. I told you I'd feel the same in the morning, and I do."

Which meant she still wanted to make love to him. He didn't know if he should jump for joy or run the hell away from her. He wrapped his arms around her waist. "Good," he said, not knowing what else to say.

"I think we should present our offer, Logan. We know what Edward Reed wants to spend—"

"So, we cut it twenty-five percent and make the offer."

"Right."

"And we go from there?" He gazed into her eyes.

"Yes."

"Agreed."

She came flush against him, her face against his heart. "Why do I feel like you're placating me?"

"I don't want to fight with you, Tess. You were right when you said I wasn't working with you. I guess I still considered this my account. Like you're just along for the ride. But that's over. From now on, we handle it together."

She snuggled in closer. "I'm cold."

He smiled and tightened his arms around her. "We could go inside, or I could just keep holding you out here."

She angled her head and kissed his chin. "How did you do it? I'm no longer angry, no longer hurt, and you're holding me just like I wanted?"

He didn't know how he'd done it either, but he congratulated himself because she was exactly where he wanted her. He brushed her lips with the tip of his tongue, wetting them thoroughly before sealing their lips together in a heart-stopping kiss. He loved kissing her. Their mouths, bodies, spirits seemed to fit. When he slid his lips against her silky mouth and his tongue met hers, a sense of perfection washed over him, as if all the planets were perfectly aligned and his world had just come into focus.

He stopped the drugging kiss to tell her, but her eyes were closed. He watched her, mesmerized. She let out a small, satisfied sigh. Logan wound his fingers into her hair. She opened misty, dark eyes.

"God, you're beautiful, Tess." He backed her against the barn wall, his body molded against hers. Dust flew around their feet. The wind seemed to have picked up, but Logan barely noticed any of it.

His hands burrowed under her shirt and cupped a lace-strapped breast. Their eyes met.

"I could make love to you right here," he said.

She encircled his waist and lifted her lips to his mouth. With her hair being blown in all directions and her eyes warm and dreamy, she was a temptation few men would be able to resist. Logan couldn't and didn't want to, even if making love to her would mean more than a fun one-night stand. He captured her lips once more and caressed her rosebud nipple with his fingers until he heard a half-whimper, half-groan from deep in her throat. If he didn't stop, he *would* take her right here.

Keeping one hand on her breast, he slowly ended the kiss.

The air blew so hard, he had to make an effort to stand upright. "Maybe we'd better go in." He had to shout over the howling wind. Tess looked around and seemed for the first time to notice the wild weather.

She nodded and gave him a concerned look. "We shouldn't be out in this. It looks bad."

He backed away from her, took her hand, and together they ran to the guest house. The wind whipped around the buildings, and they had to run with all their strength to make it to the front door. Tess stumbled a couple of times, but Logan held on to her hand and pulled her along beside him. When they pushed the door open, they were propelled inside in a flurry of dust and chilly air.

Tess let out a loud 'whew'. Her face was rosy and her eyes still dark. "I'm freezing," she said

He was breathing heavy. "Me too. Let's go upstairs."

Once they reached their bedroom doors, neither seemed to be brave enough to suggest they go into one together. They each stood in front of their respective doors, staring at each other. Logan wanted to invite her into his room. He needed to hold her close and be deep inside her. They stared at each other.

"Well, one thing's for sure," he whispered.

"What?" was her shaky reply

"What we started on the ship is far from over."

She shuddered. "I don't know what we started, Logan."

He moved away from his door and went to hers. "You know; we both know."

Truth was, he'd wanted her since the first time she walked into the office in her three-inch heels and short business suit dress. He'd blown it with her then, too, by bragging about his closing percentages. Ever since then, he'd never had a chance.

She swept soft fingertips over the tops of his forearms. "What I know is it's late. I know we're in a client's home, and I know the best thing for us to do is go to sleep. Alone."

But it wasn't what he *wanted* to do. Logan sighed. "You're right, Ms. Romero. As always." He returned to his bedroom door, opened it, and glanced at her. "I'll dream of you tonight, you know?"

She smiled. "I never knew you were so romantic and sweet."

Logan chuckled. "Sweet? You have no idea what form my dreams will take."

She arched a perfect eyebrow.

He winked and entered his bedroom while he still had the inclination to do so.

CHAPTER
FOURTEEN

N^o matter how many times Teresa tossed and turned in her bed, she kept hearing voices and the muffled sounds of hurried steps. She rubbed her eyes, trying to figure out if she was dreaming or awake.

"Apurencen! Rapido!" Voices outside her bedroom called. She was definitely awake.

Teresa kicked the light blanket off her, and sat on the edge of her bed. She picked up her cell phone and angled it to see the time. She'd only been asleep a couple of hours. It was just after four in the morning.

Again, the urgent sounds of voices and footsteps came from the hallway. She opened her bedroom door and saw that the entire household seemed to be awake, dressed in work clothes and heavy jackets.

"What's going on?" She asked Miguel, whom she recognized from dinner earlier that night.

He had a frown, but when he saw her, his face softened. "Sorry to awaken you," he said in Spanish. "The wind has blown down some of our corrals, and the sheep are loose and frightened, so we must go round them up. You will excuse me?"

"Yes, of course, I—"

"Tess?" Logan came out of his room, squinting. "What's everyone doing up?"

Miguel hurried down the stairs, where other men gathered by the front door, talking about their plan to gather the sheep and repair the wind-damaged fences and structures. Teresa listened and watched from upstairs. Logan came beside her and touched her elbow. She glanced at him, intending to tell him to wait a second and let her listen to what was going on downstairs, but the words died in her throat.

Logan was in his boxer shorts, and his long, firm torso was covered with a white tank undershirt that stretched tightly across his chest, highlighting each band of muscle. Part of each nipple was visible on the edge of the oval arm openings. Teresa realized she was openly staring at his body, so she forced herself to lift her gaze. The look of desire in his eyes was unmistakable, and all she seemed able to manage was a shaky breath.

"It's okay, Tess."

What was okay? Nothing seemed okay at the moment. She glanced downstairs again. "The wind, the sheep, I think they've got big problems."

Logan released her arm and placed both hands on the banister as he leaned down and saw for himself the small army of men gathered by the front door. "Stay here," he muttered and rushed downstairs.

Teresa hurried to her bedroom, put on a robe, and went downstairs herself.

"But I appreciate your help," Mr. Pennetti was saying to Logan.

"Are you sure?"

"Yes, we're sure," Juan Carlos snarled. "The last thing we need is someone who doesn't know what he's doing out there."

"Juan Carlos, be quiet," Pennetti frowned at his son then looked back at Logan. "Please, you and your pretty co-worker go back to sleep. Tomorrow we will meet and talk, but now we really must go."

"Sure." Logan nodded and stepped back.

The men tumbled outside, and each seemed to be swept away as soon as he stepped out of the house. Logan put his entire body weight into closing the door, then turned and gave her a grim look. "They're out of their minds. Those have to be sixty-mile-an-hour winds out there."

"Why can't they wait until the winds die down?"

He lifted both eyebrows in a perplexed expression. "I guess they're worried about the animals. Seems dangerous as hell."

Teresa shivered.

Logan noticed and right away put an arm around her. "Come on, let's get back to bed."

"I don't think I can sleep, Logan."

He kissed her temple and began walking toward the stairs, leading her. "There's nothing we can do. There's no use staying up all night waiting for them to come back."

"Aren't you worried?"

They climbed the stairs together, his arm around her back. "Yeah, I am, Tess. But I volunteered to help, and Pennetti told me to stay put, because he had plenty of men who knew what they were doing. So, that's what I'm doing."

He opened her bedroom door and walked in with her. Then he released her and stepped back.

"Are you leaving?"

He grinned devilishly. "Not if you're going to look that upset about it."

She sat on the edge of the bed, feeling ridiculous. She looked at her bare, cold feet. "I just don't think I can sleep."

"You want me to keep you company?"

The provocative way he said it made her face burn and her insides melt. All her senses sharpened as if someone had actually flipped a switch on inside her. She became conscious that she was in her bedroom with a man dressed only in boxer shorts and an undershirt. Not to mention all she had on was a thin, flimsy, short night gown under her robe. "Stop it, Logan. You're such a tease."

He laughed. "You think I'm teasing?" He crouched, placing a hand on her knee, and with the other, tipped her chin. "I know we're working and have a job to do, but, well, I'd like to spend some more time with you, Tess."

"You mean, you'd like to sleep with—"

"I'd like to make love to you, yes. On the ship, you asked me to make it special for you. I'd like to try."

His eyes were so warm, so sincere, and his words so honest, they sent a strange, thrilling sensation through her. "Now?" She nearly coughed out the word.

He smiled. "Seems like the perfect time, don't you think?" He moved his hands to her waist and untied the knot on her robe. Then his hands settled on her shoulders, where he gently pushed the terry-cloth material off, leaving her exposed in her almost transparent nightgown. "I don't want to fight with you anymore, about work, about anything. I like you, Tess. I think we can be good friends."

She did too. "But we don't agree on how to handle this account, Logan. And we *are* rivals, whether we want to be or not."

He shrugged. "We agree. We want what's best for Penguin, right?"

"Well, sure."

"Do you agree that these people know what they're doing and would be good suppliers?"

"Yes."

"Then we negotiate the best deal and get out of here."

"And when we get home?" They'd be back to competing for the same accounts.

"Nothing's gonna change between us—you know it, Tess."

He would keep browbeating her at work, driving her crazy. But then again, she didn't want him to treat her any differently than he did the others. She wanted him to compete as he always had, and then when she won, she'd know she deserved every new account she got because she was the best one for the job. She caressed his face and threaded her fingers through his hair.

His hands dropped to her waist again. He held her at arm's distance as he studied her face in a kind of intense analysis. "Except that maybe some things have already changed, haven't they, Tess?" he whispered.

She trembled and didn't know why. She wasn't cold. She wasn't frightened. Or was she? "We can't let it," she said.

"We have no choice," he said right before he took her lips, propelled her back, and settled his weight on her.

Teresa was pressed into the mattress, and Logan's kiss was nothing like the playful, seductive kisses he'd shared previously. This kiss was possessive and demanding. His mouth moved powerfully over hers. Hot lips urged hers to open, and his tongue roamed vigorously with unrestrained, raw passion, which brought both ardor and terror to the surface of Teresa's body. The hardness of not only the kiss, but his entire, tense body, shook her.

She caressed his solid back, moving up his arms where she found flexed muscles and clenched fists. She opened his hands and weaved her fingers with his.

He softened the kiss and slowly backed off, until his lips barely slid across hers. Then he lifted his head and looked into her eyes. "Tell me to leave and I will."

She shook her head, trying to ignore the frantic beat of her heart. "If you need to leave, do it. I'm not going to make that decision for you."

He sighed and lowered his forehead on her shoulder. He stayed that way for a long time until she touched his face. Then he lifted his head and smiled. "How about we lie back on this bed and I hold you for a while?"

"That sounds nice."

He rolled off her, and they did just that.

As she was falling asleep, he kissed her forehead. "I'm not sorry."

"What?" She was too tired to talk anymore.

"About us. I'm not sorry."

Hold me, Logan. I need you to hold me. I'm afraid I'm falling in love with you. She wasn't sure if she was even awake anymore. Was she actually voicing this declaration of love? She didn't know. It was best to shut up. She snuggled closer to him, and a content, dreamy feeling overtook her.

Something warm and heavy was on her breast. She stretched, opened her eyes, and looked at the hand that cupped her left breast. She threw a look over her shoulder and found Logan sleeping soundly behind her, with an arm draped across her chest. She moved, and the hand on her breast closed.

"Ouch, Logan."

He moaned and pulled her against his chest. Their bodies were molded together. She sighed. It felt wonderful.

"Morning," he whispered.

What an intimate way to wake up. "Hi."

"You weren't going to get up, were you?"

"Well—"

"Because I want you to stay put for a while longer."

"Okay." What else could she say?

He gave a deep, throaty chuckle. "If you were this agreeable at work, we'd get along one hundred percent better, you know that?"

She flipped around to face him. "You're just plain rotten, Wilde."

"I'm a man who deserves a gold medal. I held you all night while you hugged me, moved against me, drove me absolutely crazy with want, yet I let you sleep. Even though I felt like waking you up and jumping your bones, I didn't."

Teresa smiled. "I appreciate it. I was very tired."

"I probably won't be in a good mood today, I warn you. I'm a deeply frustrated man."

"I appreciate your sacrifice."

He placed a hand on her hip, his teasing expression fading. "It was no sacrifice, sweetheart. It was heaven."

His words and tone always made her feel so vulnerable, maybe because he was open and honest with his feelings. "Logan, what are you doing to me?"

"I could ask you the same question."

"I don't know what I'm doing, and if you think I do, you're wrong."

"I guess I don't either, but I do know what I want."

"Tell me what you want, Logan." But she knew the answer before it came.

He frowned. "I want to be the first man who's ever touched you. I want you to feel me inside you and know how much pleasure I can give you."

That wasn't at all what she expected him to say, but it was perfect. "I want that, too."

He pulled her closer. "Good, because I like being with you, Tess. You make me feel alive and furious and crazy with desire."

There was that honesty again. She kissed his shoulder to avoid looking into those eyes.

He tightened his embrace. "Oh, Tess. I'm tired of holding back. I gave you a whole night to rethink this. Now, I'm going to make love to you. Are you sure it's what you want?"

CHAPTER FIFTEEN

Teresa's heart pounded so hard, she was sure he could hear it. This was her chance to say no. He'd leave. He might not like it, but he *would* leave. She closed her eyes tight and searched deep inside, finding the undeniable truth, she didn't want him to leave. She wanted Logan to make love to her. She opened her eyes. "I'm sure," she whispered.

He released her and sat up in bed, looking down. He scrubbed his eyes to make sure he wasn't dreaming. But he wasn't. She was there, on the bed, her hair splayed out on the pillow. She looked delicious. His hands shook. He hadn't been this nervous about making love to a woman since he was a virgin himself. He lifted his tank shirt over his head and tossed it, then he straddled her hips. Giving her a teasing grin, he said, "You're going to attach special significance to this, given it will be your first time, are you?"

She arched an eyebrow as if challenging him like she did at work, but then she smiled and gazed at him tenderly. She ran her fingers down his stomach. "Logan, come on, of course I will."

"You will?" That's what he was afraid of.

"Of course. Even if it wasn't my first time, it will be special, because it will be my first time *with you*."

He liked this woman. "I just want us to enjoy each other, and—"

"No strings." She nodded and widened her smile. "I remember."

He bent down and kissed her lips softly, then he laughed. "I feel like one of those warning stickers: 'open at your own risk' I'm sorry."

"Get over yourself, Wilde—even though it's my first time, I'm not a starry-eyed teenager. I won't fall in love and want to be with you forever, if that's what you're worried about."

He probed deep into her eyes. "Hell, Tess, maybe I'm afraid I'll be the one to fall. What would I do then, huh?"

She caressed his face. "What *would* you do?"

He lowered his lips to hers. He was finished talking. He wouldn't do anything because he wouldn't let that happen. He didn't need anything serious in his life. He just wanted to enjoy his life. And he was going to start now, with Tess.

He lifted himself to a sitting position again and took her hands, placing them on his erect penis. She felt him tentatively through the fabric of his boxer shorts. He watched the play of expressions on her face. She looked interested and frightened and excited all at once. When her curiosity seemed to demand more, she reached inside and encircled him. He jumped. She delicately slid her fingertips down the length of his full erection, in an exploratory way that had him pulsing with unfulfilled need. He knew she needed this time to get familiar with what a man looked and felt like, so he tried to concentrate on other things. The cream color of the walls, the textured ceiling, *oh*, the wooden headboard, *oh, God*.

He covered her hands and pulled them off him for a few seconds. He lifted himself completely off her and took off his boxer shorts, then he pulled her off the bed and helped her undress. As he removed her night clothes, he dropped kisses down her exquisite body. He started with her neck, lifting her hair up and letting his lips learn the contours down to her shoulders.

At her breasts, he lingered, touching lightly at first, then as the buds hardened in his mouth, his tongue thrashed the rigid tips. She moaned and scraped her nails on the back of his head and neck, her fingers shaking. When he bit her playfully, her fingertips squeezed his shoulders. He drew his head back to look at her face. He saw the hot desire in her eyes.

"You okay, Tess?"

She pulled him against her. "No, my body feels like it's on fire."

He grinned. "It is."

He trailed his fingers over her breasts, lightly scratching her tight nipples. He watched her inhale and hold her breath, and it pleased him to know he was bringing her this tortured pleasure. But he moved past her breasts and made his hands roam down the rest of her luscious body.

She tentatively laid her hands on him. She explored every inch of his body, looking up for his reaction at every move. It drove him absolutely crazy, and it left his skin tingling as if she'd spread some magic lotion on him.

He cupped her bottom and pulled her tight against his groin so she could feel what she'd done to him. Her arms wrapped around his waist, and her eyes met his. They stared at each other for a few seconds, their breathing deep, their bodies tense, their senses heightened.

Unable to delay another second, he lifted her and laid her on the bed. He braced himself over her and looked into her eyes one last time to make sure she really wanted this. He saw slight apprehension in her eyes. "Ready?"

She leaned over, reached into the drawer on the nightstand, and pulled out a condom. She had bought some on the ship, the night she'd asked Logan to make love to her. Logan took it from her and put it on.

"Just go slow, I want you to go slow."

His arms trembled. He prayed he could do what she asked. He moved between her thighs, and when the tip of his erection touched the hot, moistness between her legs, he had to take a deep breath to keep from thrusting as hard as he could.

He kissed her sweetly and began a slow, rhythmic motion that brought him each time just a little deeper into her tight walls. Having Tess beneath him, like this, was pure heaven. He lowered his face to the enticing hollow at the base of her neck and shoulders. He settled his lips on the moist tender skin. He wanted to dip his tongue down and run it along the delicate bones outlining her shoulder blades, but he waited a moment, relishing the feeling of being partially inside her. He drew a shaky breath, and the sweet smell of strawberries assailed him. *Forbidden fruit.* The thought rushed past, and he quickly cast it aside. He sank his face further into her wild hair and inhaled again. He moved within her.

Her body slowly enveloped him, taking him deeper and deeper. Then he felt the barrier, and it felt so wrong. They belonged joined as one, connected. Nothing should ever be between them. Tess was going to be his, this first time and forever. He knew he had to thrust harder and deeper this time, and that he would hurt her, and that pained him deep inside. He kissed her again as tenderly and gently as he could, then pushed through to make them one. She cried out and clutched at his shoulders.

He stopped moving and cursed himself in a million different ways. Something so wonderful shouldn't be painful. But now he would make it up to her. He was more determined than ever to bring her pleasure.

"It's okay, Tess, honey," he whispered and began moving ever so slowly again, adjusting his angle to bring her the most enjoyment possible. He increased his rhythm and kissed her passionately. "You're so beautiful, so sweet," he breathed in her ear. He licked the tears from her face and kissed her eyes. With his hands, he tried to both soothe and arouse her, holding her, caressing, worshiping.

Soon, her breathing got heavier, and he heard sounds of pleasure coming from deep in her throat.

"Better, Tess, better?"

"Yes," she gasped. Her hands now roamed his back, and settled on his bottom, encouraging him to continue.

He was starting to see red. He closed his eyes, concentrating on her, only her. He squeezed her nipples, and when he did, he felt her release, accompanied by the spasms of her body. Her arms shot up, and she clutched at his shoulders. He kissed her face everywhere, encouraging her to relax and enjoy the feeling. Then, with a few more thrusts, he joined her in paradise, almost afraid of the intensity of the feelings shooting through his body.

He didn't move afterward, not wanting to separate from the closeness they'd shared. "You okay?" He asked.

"If you mean completely satisfied," she said quietly. "Yes."

He kissed her temple. "I'll get off in a second."

"You don't have to."

He chuckled. "I think I do eventually." He slowly lifted himself off but pulled her back into his arms immediately. So many conflicting emotions warred inside him right now. Happiness, fear, worry, even desire. Sex with Teresa was the most confusing thing that had ever happened to him. He slid his hand up and down her back, worried about her but not knowing what to say.

"That was unbelievable," she said at last.

Part of him wanted to get up and run, and another part wanted to hold her close and thank her for letting him share such a moving experience with her.

He felt himself harden again as he thought of it. She felt him, too, and her eyes widened. Not again, she seemed to be saying.

"Sorry." He smiled at her. "I want you again, but I'll wait. I know you need time to recover."

She placed her hands on his face. "You were wonderful. So kind, so gentle."

"Don't let that get out, okay?"

She laughed. "Okay."

She closed her eyes and looked like she might fall asleep. It was still early. The rest of the household would not be up until late, especially if they worked most of the night in the wind, so if she wanted to sleep, he would lie here and watch her.

***

Logan was sound asleep when Teresa awoke. She glanced at his handsome face and felt herself flush. The tenderness between her legs reminded her of where he'd been, of where he'd touched and destroyed her in more ways than one. She got up and showered. When she walked out of the bathroom, wrapped in a towel, he was sitting in bed, his back against the headboard.

"Morning," she said.

Teresa noticed how cautious he was. His smile grew slowly. "You look terrific."

"I feel terrific," she said.

"Glad to hear it."

He stood, magnificently naked, walked to her, and gave her a tentative kiss.

"I don't regret it, Logan." Being in his arms had been as wonderful as she'd known it would be. He was strong and gentle at the same time, and he made love as if he adored her. Who could ask for a better lover?

"Glad to hear that too."

She placed her hands on his firm, smooth chest, feeling his heartbeat beneath her palms. "Don't let it go to your head, but you were perfect. You made it more than special for me."

He threaded his fingers through her hair. "And you're absolutely beautiful, Tess."

She smiled. "Does this feel as awkward to you as it does to me?"

"I guess it does." He eased her hand off his chest. "My turn in the shower?"

She stepped aside. "Yes, go ahead."

He gave her a fleeting kiss as he escaped her room. The fun was over, Teresa thought, and tried not to let it bother her. She sighed as she watched him walk away. Logan had a long, solid torso that seemed to stretch out forever before tapering to his narrow hips. He was gorgeous. He reminded her of those thin, sexy rock stars she used to drool over when she watched music videos as a teenager. Logan wasn't just a sexy image on TV, though; he was flesh and blood, and deeply in her system, more than she dared admit.

***

The scalding water fell on his head and back and stung his skin. He felt the corded muscle on his back tense as he braced his fisted hands on the tile of the shower wall. Making love to Teresa had been earth-shattering.

The shower stall filled with steam, and his skin grew numb. If only that numbness would seep right through to his heart, and keep it from beating such an abnormal rhythm. But he found when it came to Teresa, he had as little control over his feelings lately as he did his body. He turned on the cold water, allowing the shower to rain warm.

He tipped his face back and closed his eyes. Maybe if he stood under here long enough, he could regain his self-control. Teresa was getting under his skin, that much was true, but that should be a good thing. He liked her . . . a lot. Then why was he terrified?

"Logan? Getting out soon?"

He opened his eyes and stared through the foggy, glass, shower door. Teresa was on the other side. She was still wrapped in that towel and looked marvelous even through an obstructed barrier. Suddenly he felt like laughing at himself. He was afraid of her? A wonderful, loving woman?

"Why don't you come in?" He asked.

"Oh, no. I've had my shower, thank you very much. I need to do my hair and makeup."

He chuckled, soaped himself, rinsed, and shut the water off. As he stepped out of the shower he grabbed and kissed her. "Chicken."

She caressed his face, then softly touched her lips to his again. His heart began that song again. He let her go and grabbed a towel, hastily rubbing his head, then wrapping it around his hips.

"Logan?"

"What?"

"Thanks for staying with me last night."

"You don't have to thank me. I wanted to stay."

She glanced away, but stood rooted where she was for a few seconds. Then she flashed him a bright smile before turning her attention to the mirror. He felt like he should have said more, like she was expecting more, but he didn't know what to say. He walked away, feeling like a fool—he just made love to the woman—yet he didn't know what to say to her.

***

At breakfast, Logan asked Pennetti about the wind damage, and about the men who left last night. A couple of guys had been hurt. The wind had caused a black out and they couldn't see chunks of wood and other debris coming at them. They were taken to the local clinic. The rest of the men were tired, scratched or bruised, but otherwise, okay.

"Do you mind if we postpone negotiations until tonight or tomorrow? We still have a lot of clean up to do today, so I need to get back out there."

Logan shrugged. He could definitely understand that. "Not a problem. Mind if we tag along?"

"Of course not, that would be fine."

Logan and Teresa took a jeep with Manuel Pennetti to see the sheep corals. Logan sat up front with Pennetti while Teresa sat alone in the back. She hadn't said much during breakfast, and as he glanced back now, her face was lifeless and her eyes seemed glazed over.

"What are you staring at?" He asked.

She had no reaction, didn't seem to hear him. He reached back and touched her knee. That got her attention; her eyes darted to his hand, then to his face. He smiled. She smiled back.

The bouncing of the jeep and the wind, which still blew with enough force to whip the jeep over the road, made conversation difficult, so he faced forward again.

Men on horseback and sheep dogs continued to herd sheep into enclosed areas, while other men lifted planks of wood and hammered fences together.

Pennetti stopped his jeep and jumped out. Logan hurried to follow him then glanced back and offered his hand to Teresa.

"I'm right behind you," she said, but sat in the jeep and watched Logan and Manuel Pennetti stride away. Teresa reclined in the seat, enjoying the cool, crisp wind drifting across her face. The land down here was brutal but beautiful. At a distance, the snow-capped peeks of the Andes mountains were visible, and Teresa wished she and Logan were here under different circumstances.

The truth was, however, they were here to get a job done. They'd gotten seduced by the vacation-like trip on the ship, and now this ranch where they were treated like guests. Since she'd left home, she'd let her emotions and desires guide her, and she'd acted out of character. Something told her she'd pay dearly for that slip.

Teresa wished her sister were here so she could talk her feelings over with her, but even if Carla were here, Teresa probably wouldn't tell her a thing. What would she say? *I agreed to a casual affair with my co-worker, but now I'm having feelings that aren't casual at all.* No, she couldn't tell anyone. She had to stop being ridiculous, wrap up negotiations, and get back home to her other accounts.

She watched the men repair the shredded fences, hastily hammering together planks of wood. Around noon, she returned to the ranch house and asked the cooks to prepare some food for the men. She helped pack water and wine, then drove back out to deliver the care package to the men. Logan sat beside her, sweaty, dirty, and incredibly sexy looking. She did her best to keep her eyes off him.

"Senor Pennetti—"

"Manuel, please."

"Manuel, we need to discuss the wool purchase. Is tonight possible?"

"Yes, Logan and I have been talking about it. We may have come to an understanding."

She glanced at Logan, who smiled, his mouth full of a beef steak sandwich.

"I see," she said, wondering what they talked about. "Well, then, we can put it all on paper tonight."

"That is good, Señorita."

She didn't ask Logan what the two of them had discussed, figuring he'd fill her in in private. She noticed the scowl on Juan Carlos' face and concluded he, too, needed to be filled in on this talk between Manuel Pennetti and Logan Wilde.

CHAPTER
SIXTEEN

Teresa disappeared after lunch. She took the jeep and headed back to the estancia, and he returned to the corrals to finish the repair jobs. Although he was surrounded by other men all day, his thoughts were only on Teresa. When they finished working for the day, his only desire had been to hurry back to his room, shower, and go see her.

Logan knocked on Teresa's door as a warning before opening it and peeking inside. "Tess?"

She sat cross-legged on her bed, staring at the screen on her laptop. "Yes?" she said without looking up.

He strolled in, aware of every muscle behind his legs and on his back. It had been a while since he'd done this much physical work, but he liked it. It was better than sitting behind a desk. The warm shower helped ease the tightness, but he knew he'd be sore for a few days.

He stood beside Teresa's bed waiting for her to look up, but she didn't. "Am I interrupting?"

"Yes," she muttered.

"Yes?"

She glanced up absently and shook her head. "Sorry, no. I've graphed the average fiber length, strength, and diameter size and compared them to the stats from the American Sheep Industry Association."

Logan sat on the bed beside her, leaning his upper body weight on his tired arm. So that was what she'd been doing all day?

"See here." She pointed at the screen.

Logan studied her colorful graphs. Damn, she was precise. "What's your standard deviation?"

"Three point seven microns."

He nodded and turned to look at her profile. She had reading glasses down low on her nose, and a slight frown wrinkling the spot between her brows. Her face was clean of makeup. Her lips were full and tempting like always. But she didn't even know he was sitting beside her. He could have been anyone she was doing business with.

"Not bad, huh?" She said and tilted her face toward his.

"Not bad," he agreed, peering into her large brown eyes.

She held his gaze for a few moments, then her lids lowered, and as if they were lasers, he felt her eyes examine his lips, chin, and chest, exposed by the open shirt he had thrown on, then lower to his jeans. Blood coursed through his worn-out body, making parts of him come alive with renewed vivacity. As if jolted, her focus shot back up to his eyes. "How did it go out there?"

Finally, she acknowledged he was there beside her. "I'm worn out."

She lowered her eyes again, but this time she was deliberately not looking at him. "I'm sure they appreciated your help. Should I print out this micron report for our meeting?"

He reached for her wrist and captured it. Then he caressed the soft inner skin. "Naw, don't get up."

She glanced at his hand that restrained her, then back at him. She took a deep breath. "I called Edward today and told him we're wrapping things up tonight and should be back home by next week."

Logan felt his heart drop. What happened? Why was she all business again? He knew he should have said more this morning, held her longer, something. "You shouldn't have done that," he said.

She eased her wrist out of his grip. "I thought he should know how we're doing. He sounded pleased."

"You don't know how negotiations will go. We may be here longer."

She shook her head. "The only flight out of here for the next week and a half is in two days. We've got to wrap things up by then."

He watched the hard determination on her face. Her entire body was tense and rigid, except her lips—they never looked hard. They were always lush and sweet-looking. "What's the hurry, Tess?"

She shrugged. "We just need to do what we came here to do and get back to our other accounts, that's all."

Right. That was far from all. "It can't hurt to spend some more time and really check things out well. Once we all sign on the dotted line, it's over, we're all working together."

"That's why I spent all day and evening running tests and coming up with quality analysis."

He smiled. Her mind was made up. But he had to know if she was running away from him. Tess was honest; she'd tell him if he asked. "I guess we're ready to negotiate then."

She nodded, her lips inching up in a sorry excuse for a smile. "What time?"

"Pennetti said after dinner."

"Okay."

"Now, Tess, about us."

"Us?" She looked like one of the frightened sheep from this afternoon.

Her reaction bothered him. Maybe she was having the same scary feelings he was. Maybe she was getting too close. The closeness itself wasn't bothersome, but he didn't want to complicate their relationship. They worked together after all. They could get together, have some fun, and share a few laughs, but nothing serious; that would only create problems.

Still, he couldn't help himself. He reached up and slipped his fingers behind her neck and kissed the lips he'd been staring at since he walked into her room. "I can't get enough of you," he admitted.

She stared at his lips, looking like she might cry any minute. "But you're wishing you could; I saw it in your eyes today. You don't want to want me."

That wasn't true. He didn't mind wanting her. But he knew what she meant, and he liked her too much to play games. He let her go. "No, I don't. Not the way I have in the past few days. All I *want* is to be with you, to talk to you, watch you, make love to you. I sure as hell don't want to be this preoccupied with you, you're right, Tess."

Her eyes had been glued on him, and now they turned away. She clicked her program off and closed the laptop shut. She uncrossed her silky, smooth, coffee-colored legs, and slid them over the side of the bed opposite him. "Then it's a good thing we'll be wrapping things up here and going home."

"Tess." He got up, feeling miserable. He didn't want to hurt her.

She placed her laptop on a desk and smiled when she faced him again. "Don't. I feel an apology coming on, and you have nothing to apologize for. I've come to value our friendship, and I'm grateful we've been able to work together."

He rubbed the back of his neck, looking at her from the top rim of his eyes. "I wasn't going to apologize." He walked up to her and threaded fingers of both hands into her hair. "I was going to say that although I don't want to feel these things about you, Tess, I do. Every time I'm with you, I want more of you, not less."

She slipped her hands inside his open shirt. Soft, loving hands slid up the length of his rib cage on both sides. Her caress on his bare skin was pure heaven. He touched her lips with his, just a slight touch to feel her warm breath on his mouth. He stood a full head taller than her, and he loved it, because when she kissed him, she had to stretch her lovely neck to look up at him.

Her hands slid to his back, moving over muscles which had complained earlier of the straining work. Now, his back felt the heat of her hands, and they had an almost healing effect. She'd stepped closer, so he pressed his lips harder against hers. He caressed her lips while she stroked his back with her hands. He withdrew momentarily, then with his tongue he traced her luscious red lips.

"Oh Logan," she sighed.

Then he closed his mouth over hers, taking a real kiss with all the passion and emotion he had bottled up inside him. He plunged his tongue inside her mouth and ground his lips against hers. She kissed him back just as passionately, just as aggressively.

Logan didn't ever want to stop touching this woman. He took her shoulders and pushed her back against the desk, but she protested. Her wondrous hands moved to his stomach and prevented him from getting closer. Logan raised his head and peered into her eyes. "Like I said, I can't help myself."

Teresa touched her lips with her fingertips. She shook her head. "Please leave. We have a meeting to get ready for, and I can't think when you're around."

Logan smiled. He felt an inexplicable possessiveness he'd never felt about any other woman. "I'll just have to make sure I stay close by then."

***

If Tess was distracted, not a soul could have guessed. True to her tigress reputation, once the library doors closed and negotiations officially began, she charged her prey and mercilessly pursued. She outlined Penguin's plan and its vision for the new wool products, as well as how *El Gaucho Estancia* would fit into the future.

Pennetti seemed disoriented, and Logan crossed his legs and watched her operate. He was impressed. Juan Carlos, however, did not seem at all affected. As soon as Tess finished addressing her points, he leaned forward in his chair and eyed Logan.

"You agree with Teresa?"

"Of course," Logan said without hesitation. *Always show a united front.*

Juan Carlos nodded. "I thought so. When Teresa and I discussed this before, I met with my father and we—"

"What do you mean when you and Teresa discussed this *before*? When was this?" Logan glanced from Juan Carlos to Teresa.

Juan Carlos shot him a smug grin. "You mean she didn't tell you? It was a few nights ago when you came looking for her in the barn."

Tess looked only mildly uneasy. "We discussed the benefits for the estancia if Penguin were to use them, that's all, Logan."

Logan pinned her with a look he only hoped would convey how furious he was. Then he turned his attention to Juan Carlos, suspiciously fearing Juan Carlos now had the upper hand. "So did you agree with her assessment?"

"Teresa is a very bright woman."

Logan hated the way he used her name so intimately. He should be calling her Ms. Romero, but it wasn't up to Logan to correct him. "That, she is."

"She knows that a competent operation like ours can get you all the raw materials you'll need for your new products. She also knows that you can get it for a steal."

Logan shrugged. "We're willing to offer you a fair deal."

Juan Carlos shook his head. "Not fair to us. You will make demands on us that will force us to mold to the way you do business. You will own us."

"We'll be your largest customers," Logan agreed.

"Yes, and we will become dependent on you. We will not be able to handle other accounts and meet your needs concurrently, so we will be stuck with only you. Then you will hold too much control over our future."

Logan turned to Teresa. "Where's our offer?"

She handed him a sheet of paper. Logan read the offer. It was a fair financial offer in exchange for expected yearly supplies of wool. Juan Carlos was right about one thing: Penguin would expect them to perform and deliver on schedule. If Pennetti had other commitments, he'd have to work them around Penguin's shipments.

"That's our offer, Señor Pennetti," Logan addressed the older man. "If you think it's too much for your farm, we understand. We need your complete loyalty and cooperation, and if you view that as owning you, then perhaps Penguin is just too large an account for you."

"Do not be offended by my son, Mr. Wilde. He wants what is best for our family."

Logan nodded. "I thought we all did."

"Maybe so." Pennetti smiled. "But I have to respect my son's opinion. We have to decide if it is best for us to have one large account or many small. We will discuss it and let you know in a day or so."

"We leave in two days," Teresa said, looking as sick about this turn of events as Logan felt.

"Very well, tomorrow then."

CHAPTER
SEVENTEEN

T eresa followed Logan out, knowing he was going to be all over her for talking with Juan Carlos before negotiations started. He was going to blame her for tonight's disaster, and he'd be right.

Logan climbed the stairs two at a time without even waiting to see if she was behind him. He went into his bedroom and slammed the door. Teresa stood outside in the hallway, wondering if she ought to follow him in or not. Finally, she decided she needed to talk to him. They needed to discuss their next steps. She opened his door. He stood with his hands on his hips, staring out the window into the darkness. His back was stiff.

"Logan?" She entered and closed the door behind her.

In a move that was so quick she barely had a chance to be shocked, he slammed the wall with his open palm. "That damn, arrogant, S.O .B. I knew he was going to be trouble."

Teresa took a tentative step forward. "He's just bluffing. He wants to throw us off so we'll offer him whatever he wants."

Logan turned around, his face could have been carved in stone. Only his Adam's apple bobbed up and down convulsively. "No. We're out of here, Tess. I can't trust that bastard."

"Logan—"

"It's over."

"Are you crazy? When they see we're not budging and that we've offered them a fair deal, they'll accept. This is the way the game is played. You can't give up so easily."

Logan moved closer. His expression softened, and he slid the back of his fingers down the side of her face. "Normally that's the way it goes, yes, but I have a bad feeling here. Juan Carlos doesn't want us. We can't enter into a contract with someone like that."

Teresa did her best to ignore the fluttering in her stomach caused by his touch. "He doesn't like the trend of Argentines selling their industries and businesses to foreigners."

Logan frowned. "That doesn't make any sense."

"I know it, but that's what he told me. I'm sorry, this is my fault. I should have told you what we talked about earlier."

He stared at her without blinking. "You should have, Tess."

But her mind had been occupied with Logan. She looked down at her feet. "Oh God, I blew it. He used what we talked about to convince his father that they don't need us."

Logan scooped his hand under hers and held her open hand in his. Large fingers caressed her inner wrist. "Which is precisely why we don't want to do business with him. You didn't do anything wrong."

She tilted her head, looking at him from the corners of her eyes. A few days ago, he would have been all over her for the slightest mistake. "What's Edward Reed going to say if we come back without this account?"

He stopped his maddening caress and wrapped his long fingers around her wrist, tugging, bringing her closer to his warm body. With his other hand, he gripped her other wrist. He held her in front of him, staring down, an earnest expression on his face. "He's gonna be pissed."

Logan bent his head, angling it enough to bequeath baby kisses along her jawline. He let out a shuddering breath above her ear. "Don't worry, baby. We did our job."

Teresa closed her eyes, sliding her face against his, enjoying the scent of soap and spice on his skin. When her lips glided across his, she opened her eyes and gazed at his handsome face. "Did we?" she whispered. "How?"

"We checked things out and concluded it's not in Penguin's best interest to contract with Pennetti," Logan said with much more conviction than she would have.

Part of her wanted to cry. She didn't like to fail. Everything was supposed to go smoothly. How could they fail? She stared at Logan's lips. Neither one had been at their best. They'd been engrossed in each other rather than focused on their job. They'd acted unprofessionally, and now they were going to lose the account. She shifted her vision to his eyes.

He forced her still manacled wrists behind her back as he wrapped his arms around her, and crushed his lips to hers. The kiss was delivered savagely, almost painfully. She felt deliciously trapped as she returned the kiss.

He released her wrists and cupped her bottom, pulling her against the stiff arousal in his pants. Her hands lay limp at her sides momentarily until she managed to plant them on his hips and hold on for dear life as he filled her with wildly erotic desires. The suggestive nature of his movements warmed her entire body.

"Logan," she managed the breathy word. "We can't."

"Shhh." He slowly eased up and eventually let her slide down gently against his body. He breathed heavy, but his body stilled. When his breathing returned to normal, he released her.

"You'll back me when I tell them the deal is off tomorrow."

She didn't want to lose the account. There was still hope. They could work things out. Juan Carlos would give in; he just wanted to hold on to some power. The machismo in him needed to believe things had worked in his favor. The Argentine male shared this immature, face-saving, muscle-flexing attitude with his Mexican cousins. "You're overreacting. Give them a chance."

"Damn it, Tess. I need your—"

"All right," she said immediately. "I'll back you." Maybe *all* males suffered from the same macho disease. But she wasn't going to argue with Logan right now. "Tell me what you want me to do."

He smiled. "Just give it up, Tess. There'll be other accounts."

She was profoundly disappointed, and she also realized that her commission had just gone down to zero, and she'd have no money to give her parents. "I know," she said. But she wasn't so sure.

Logan could see in her eyes that she was blaming herself, and although he felt she made a big mistake talking to anyone but Pennetti, there was no point in saying anything that would make her feel any worse. Besides, Juan Carlos had made up his mind about selling to Penguin long before they got there. Too bad he hadn't said anything to his father before Penguin spent so much time and money sending Logan and Teresa down here.

Logan took hold of her hand. "Let's go."

"Where?" She planted her heels.

"You've still got the keys to that jeep?"

"Yes, but—"

"Good, let's go for a ride."

"It's after midnight," she argued.

Logan smiled. He was beginning to like that she questioned him about everything. That personality trait made her different from every other woman he knew. Most women were more than happy to accommodate him and his whims without question. "That's true. It's a good thing there are plenty of flashlights in the Jeep from last night."

Teresa was tired, discouraged, and in no mood to go tromping through the deserted Patagonia in the middle of the night, but she followed this crazy man anyway. Since they started this trip, she'd been doing things she'd never done before, and she had to admit, not a boring moment passed when she was with Logan.

They climbed into the Jeep, and Logan began driving. Luckily, no wind blew tonight. He headed toward a distant mountain. "Are you going to tell me where we're going?"

He shook his head and flashed her an adorable sideways grin. "Naw, I'm going to keep you in suspense."

The night was beautiful. Teresa rested her head back and admired the open, velvety sky, not one cloud thwarted the view of the glorious star-studded heavens. She felt, at once, insignificant below all that vastness, and filled with an awesome sense of belonging to something much greater.

Logan turned sharply to the left and summoned her attention back to their destination. They came to a rocky mountain and Logan stopped the Jeep.

She looked around, feeling nervous. "Are we here?"

"Yep, grab a couple of flashlights."

"This is creepy."

"Don't worry, I'll protect you," he said and laughed.

He pulled her hand and led her down a narrow trail alongside the mountain. "Come on, Logan, I'm getting scared. Let's get out of here."

He ignored her and turned into something that looked like a cave. She imagined all types of things inside, from real beasts like bats and tarantulas to imaginary creatures like three-headed trolls.

"What the hell are we doing here?" She asked in a shaky voice, inching closer to him.

"This is Chavez's Cave. The guys told me about it today. There's supposed to be some petroglyphs inside."

"Wonderful, so I'm risking my life in some cold, damp, dark cave to see some rock-carvings."

He hooked his arm around her waist and kissed her neck, sending a different kind of chill ripping through her. "Relax, Tess, this is supposed to be fun."

"I'm not having any yet."

"Nothing's gonna hurt you, I promise. Look! Point your flashlight this way."

He released her and illuminated a wall filled with brownish ostrich-looking birds, red handprints, and something that looked like a dartboard. It gave her an eerie feeling.

Logan placed a warm hand on the back of her neck. "Cool, huh?"

She nodded. She'd seen pictographs before, but never in the middle of the night with a man who brought a radiance to everything he did. Her heart picked up speed.

"The ranch hands said the natives out here liked to do these hand paintings. There's another cave further north called 'Cave of the Painted Hands' because of the hundreds of these hand representations."

"I wonder what they meant?"

"Who knows?"

They walked back out to the clear night, hand in hand. Teresa was continually amazed at the different facets of Logan's personality. He could be annoyingly lackadaisical about work one moment and the next so competent it would throw her for a loop. Bringing her to see pictographs, alone at night with flashlights, was just another unexpected, thrilling part of him she loved.

They got back in the Jeep and he drove to a nearby lake. He parked beside the lake, put his feet up on the dash, and leaned back in the driver's seat. The moon was so bright it was like a spotlight.

"Thanks for that."

His hands cradled his head. He rolled it to look at her. "I don't want a failed account to be the last thing you take away from here. It's just an account, not the end of the world. You take life too seriously."

"It upsets you too, don't pretend it doesn't."

"Sure. I think Juan Carlos is a jerk, but we'll work with someone else. It's only a setback."

An expensive one, Teresa thought. She scooted beside him. He enfolded her in the crook of his arm, and she lay her head on his shoulder.

"But this is"—he kissed her temple—"what it's all about." They lay together looking out at the lake, stars, and the moon. Teresa could stay like this forever.

He began to kiss her ear, face, and neck. She released a shaky breath and angled her face to join her lips to his.

He granted her a small kiss, then pulled back, giving her a penetrating look. "Why me, Tess?"

She wasn't sure what he was asking. "Why. . . ?" She shook her head and frowned.

"You waited all those years for the right guy, and then you made love to me. Why?"

Because you're the right guy. She focused on his chin, knowing that was the last thing he wanted to hear. She shrugged. "I didn't plan to wait. It just kind of happened."

His fingers played with her hair, making it difficult for her to concentrate. "That's hard to believe."

"I've dated a lot, but nothing serious. I spent most of my time studying or working. The older I got, the harder it became to just casually jump in bed with someone."

He moved his hand from her hair and was now outlining her ear, ever so slowly. "You're just not the casual sex kind of girl, Tess, admit it."

No, she wasn't. She'd finally tried it and ended up losing her heart along with her virginity. She reached up and buried her fingers in *his* silky hair. "I'm admitting nothing, Wilde." She already felt too vulnerable with him.

His fingertips slid down her jawline to her lips. His eyes were hooded; he'd taken in every line, every blemish of her face. She felt completely exposed to him. She didn't need to admit anything. It was all there, open for him to see. He tipped her chin in an unexpected move and angled his head as if he were going to kiss her, but he just hovered above her lips. His eyelids flipped up, and intense brown eyes connected with hers.

"I don't mind admitting I liked making love to you for the first time, Tess." From behind his other hand settled heavily on her belly. His touch sent intense heat to her highly sensitive skin. "I liked that I was the first man to ever touch you that way. I loved having you experience desire and pleasure while I was buried deep inside you."

Teresa's breath was coming unevenly now. She couldn't stare into his eyes anymore. She closed her eyes and settled her head back on his shoulders again.

"I loved that it was all new to you," he continued to whisper in her ear. His fingers lowered to her abdomen, where he unbuttoned her slacks and slid down the zipper. Slowly, he lowered his hand under her panties. "I don't mind admitting I enjoyed seducing you and making you lose control."

He was caressing her sensitive center in a maddening rhythm. Teresa didn't realize it was possible for another human being to touch her so deliciously. He repeatedly brought her to the brink of falling apart, then backed off. His touch drove Teresa so wild that she begged for fulfillment. He gave her a throaty laugh, unzipped his jeans, then proceeded to help her out of her pants and teach her how to straddle him. His hands guided her hips. Her wet, willing body took him in, and he delivered the sexiest moan she'd ever heard. This time, there was no pain, only pleasure, for both of them.

"I think what I loved the best was that you surrendered yourself to me so unconditionally, so sweetly," he said between gasps.

The ecstasy of their movement of love increased to a fevered pitch until it fragmented Teresa's senses and left her limp and exhausted on Logan's lap. She was dazed, unable to lift her head off his shoulder.

His hands were under her shirt, and he methodically glided his fingers on her bare back. "Oh, Tess ..."

Teresa waited for him to say more. He'd talked so much, yet he still hadn't said what she wanted to hear. She needed so badly to have him express something tender, and she felt he wanted to. She, herself, felt something tight and unfamiliar in her chest. "Logan, I loved that." She lifted her head and looked at his face. He wore a dark, unfamiliar expression. "Logan?"

He gripped her upper arms and pried her back. "Admit it. Lovemaking is special to you. That's why you waited."

She wanted to caress his face, but he held her arms hostage. Why did he want her to confess something he didn't want to hear? Something he wasn't able to reciprocate. "I decided to make love to *you* because you're kind and honest. You make me laugh, you're sexy, you turn me on, and you made me feel beautiful. I made love to *you* because you made me want to. It's that simple."

He slowly nodded. 'Okay, good enough." Then he shifted her off him and began to take her remaining clothes off.

"What are you doing?"

"The water in that lake is going to be cold, but it will feel great, come on."

She followed him into the icy water but could only stay in for a few minutes. She came out shivering, but refreshed. Logan quickly wrapped her in his shirt and pulled her into the back seat of the Jeep. He positioned himself over her, and she realized he intended to make love to her again. He was as hard and erect as if he hadn't had sex in days. Teresa sighed. He was spectacular.

"Keep following me, Tess," he said as he pushed inside her. Her body took him in and she gasped. "I have so much more I want to show you."

Logan made love as good-naturedly as he did everything else, and it seemed perfectly natural to be naked in the back of a Jeep, having sex with him. She allowed herself to touch him, learn about him, and herself unselfconsciously. With others, she might have been shy, maybe even ashamed to seek gratification as greedily as she did, but not with Logan. She arched her body, seeking more. But he approached, even lovemaking, with a lazy attitude. He had no plan, no agenda, he did what came naturally and encouraged her to do the same. His only goal was enjoyment. Every stroke, every kiss, every nibble brought her closer to release, but he prolonged it, made her wait, made her savor it. When it came, she screamed out his name, and he held her tight. "That was perfect," he said. "Absolutely perfect."

They stayed out by the lake until the sun came up a couple of hours later. Teresa was exhausted, but she'd spent the most beautiful night of her life out there with Logan, and she wouldn't have traded it for anything, even sleep.

They sat on the edge of the lake, noticing for the first time, the duck-like birds on the water. Not a soul was around.

He leaned over and kissed the side of her neck, gentler and more loving than she'd ever expected from him. "I had a great time," he said and flipped over on his back so his head lay on her lap.

She combed her fingers repeatedly through his hair. "Me too."

"Teresa."

"What?"

"You were counting on the commission from this account to give to your parents, weren't you?"

The question was so unexpected, and so far from her mind at the moment, she stared at him and stopped playing with his hair. "How did you know that?"

The corners of his lips lifted gently. "I didn't. I assumed."

She looked out at the birds on the lake. "My parents are too proud to accept money from me, so I'm officially supposed to be *lending* them enough to pay half of their debts by next month. Even that would have only alleviated the problem a little. It looks like I'm not going to be able to keep my promise. Maybe *I'll* take out a loan to pay theirs."

"That's a good idea—a loan from me."

She glanced down at her lap again, where his head rested comfortably. "From you?"

"I'd like to lend you the money. Interest-free."

She shook her head. "No, no way, you're not giving me—"

"You're right, I'm *lending* you the money, not giving."

She was about to protest again when he raised his hands and sandwiched her face between them, forcing her to look at him.

"You're my friend. I enjoy helping my friends. Besides, I know where you work. It's not like you're going to run off with the money."

"It just doesn't feel right."

He released her face and smiled. "Neither does making your parents file for bankruptcy and close the restaurant. Take the money, Tess. I don't need it right now."

Tears sprang to her eyes. "I don't know what to say. Thank you seems so inadequate."

"Works for me."

She moved four fingers along his chin and forehead, loving him so much. "You're too good to be true, Logan."

His face was a picture of mixed emotions. She saw pain, happiness, desire, embarrassment, and all in a flash of a second, before he closed his eyes. "It's no big deal."

"Look at me."

He opened his eyes again and sat up. He hugged his knees and stared at her. "I wish I still had parents to help out when they needed me. I don't. So don't thank me for doing something as trivial as lending you money."

Trivial? She smiled at him. "Okay, but I'll pay you back. I promise."

He hooked his hand behind her neck. As he began to kiss her, Teresa never felt more loved. And she knew, beyond any doubt, she was in love with Logan.

He pulled back and smiled. "Maybe someday, when we get home, you'll let me make love to you again."

Someday? He talked as if it was over between them, and she thought it was just beginning. "If you want," she said, disappointed he wasn't begging her to let him in her bed every night from now on.

He smiled crookedly. "If I want? Lady, you'd better be careful what you say. I might want more than you're willing to give."

He could have her anytime he wanted. She'd give him anything, everything if he looked at her with those absorbing brown eyes the way he was now. As she watched his smiling face, she almost told him the craziness going through her head, but luckily caught herself.

Wouldn't he just love to hear how pathetic she was? A guy sleeps with her, and she's willing to turn over body and soul to him. "You're right," she said and forced herself to smile back at him. "I'd better be careful."

And she was. Careful not to show her disappointment when they told Pennetti they would not do business with *El Gaucho Estancia* after all; careful to hide her new feelings for Logan on the long plane ride home. As for Logan, he slept for most of the trip back, saying very little when he was awake. The distance between them was visible. She prayed that she'd be able to face him every day and maintain a casual work relationship. The sharp ache in her heart told her she was a liar and a fool if she expected to pull that off.

CHAPTER EIGHTEEN

Logan made sure to be in the office early, before Edward came in. He got the report typed, placed it on Edward's desk, and sat to wait for him.

Edward came in after a few minutes. "Welcome back." He smiled as he placed his briefcase on his desk. He pulled up his pants, which were always sagging. He'd gotten skinnier in his old age, but hadn't replaced his wardrobe in the past twenty years. "You look tired. How did it go?"

"Report's on your desk."

Edward sat, picked it up, and began to read. Logan remained slouched in the chair opposite Edward, watching his face transform from cheerful to surprised to angry. Then he lowered his hand and set the report on his desk and faced Logan. "Is this a joke?"

"'Fraid not."

"You mean to tell me, I've got a new line of clothes coming out next season and no supplier?"

Logan straightened in his seat and leaned forward. "We'll get someone else."

Edward's face reddened. "I sent you down there to close the deal. What the hell happened?"

"You sent me there to verify that we wanted to do business with Pennetti's company. Trust me, they were all wrong for us."

"Bull—that's not what Tess told me over the phone. Where is she, by the way?"

Logan slouched back again and rubbed his right temple. "I'm sure she'll be here any minute, and what she told you over the phone was only part of the story. The wool quality was good, the operation well run, but—"

"Exactly, so where's the damn contract, Logan?"

Logan sighed. He explained the problem with Juan Carlos, his reluctance to do business with a foreign company, his unfair demands. He didn't mention Tess. But Edward was too perceptive.

"What about Teresa? Couldn't she talk some sense into the man?"

Logan shook his head. "I didn't want her dealing with that jerk."

Edward lifted an eyebrow. "You didn't want her *dealing* with him. That's what she was supposed to do."

"Look, she tried; we both tried."

"Tried. I send my two best buyers and they 'try'," he said to himself. "I thought you were the perfect team."

"We were the perfect team. We did our job, Edward. You're still free to work with them but know it'll be against our recommendation."

"You and Tess did work together, right? You didn't spend the whole time fighting?"

"We got along great. She's a wonderful woman."

Edward continued to give him a questioning stare. "Wonderful? Teresa? What the hell happened between you two?"

Logan didn't want to talk about Tess. He broke eye contact.

Edward cursed. "And here I thought if I sent you to Argentina with *her*, you'd be forced to work, considering her 'all business' reputation. You had no business getting involved with her, Logan."

"Probably not," Logan admitted, trying to ignore the rising anger inside.

"If you wanted to add her to your list of conquests, you should have waited until you got home."

Logan felt a sickening weight in his stomach. It wasn't like that with Tess. He lowered his eyes, trying to assuage his own guilt. When the trip started, hadn't he thought of Tess in exactly that manner, a challenge? "What happened between us is none of your business," he said as he stared at his sneakers.

"The hell it isn't. When you spend your time trying to get into her pants instead of closing this account, it is my business, damn it." Edward's face was bright red.

Logan wanted to get up and scream right back at him. He wanted to tell Edward that he hadn't listened to a word Logan had said, and that he was being unfair, but the words wouldn't come out. All he could do was stare at Edward and silently admit that Edward was partly right. His mind had been on Teresa most of the time. He'd seen an opportunity to get close to her and had obsessively focused on her instead of the account.

"You sent me with her because you thought she'd have nothing to do with me? So I'd be forced to concentrate on work," he mumbled to himself.

"This was an important account for us. So, yes, I wanted you to concentrate on the account, not your partner."

He angled his face and looked at Edward from the corner of his eyes. He'd sent Teresa to babysit him, to make sure he got his work done. "Well, your plan backfired. I had a hard time concentrating on anything but Tess."

***

Teresa was still adjusting to being back in the U.S. Her sleep schedule was all off, and she felt disoriented, but she managed to walk into work on time anyway.

Krystle was the first one to greet her, of course, before she even got to her desk. "How did it go? Was it absolutely awesome? Logan said the scenery was out of this world and—"

"Logan's in already?" Teresa placed her purse in the bottom desk drawer.

"He was here bright and early, and I must say we were all surprised to see him in one piece. We were sure you'd have torn him to bits."

Boy, they thought well of her here. She attempted a halfhearted smile, but it died halfway through. "Where is he?"

"Logan? In with Mr. Reed. Were you able to work together, or was it just miserable?"

Did she have a second job with the tabloid magazines because she was good? "We got along fine, Krystle. We're co-workers for goodness sake." She looked at Edward's closed door. Should she go in, or would she be interrupting?

"Do you think he got here first to kiss up to Mr. Reed and make it seem like he did most of the work?"

Teresa returned her eyes to Krystle. They were all sharks, every one of them. When they smelled blood, they swarmed, ready to take their own bite of the victim. "I . . . I'm really tired." She was too distracted to think straight this morning.

"What coffee? There's fresh brew in the pot."

She glanced at the coffee pot, then at Edward's closed door again. "No, thanks, Krystle. I'd better get in there, thanks." She patted Krystle on the shoulder and moved around her desk. Her head started to pound.

Teresa cracked Edward's door and peeked in. Both men glanced at the door.

"Tess! We've been waiting for you. Come in," Edward said immediately

Logan smiled politely, but didn't say a word. She took a seat in the chair beside him.

"Logan was filling me in on the trip. It seems things didn't go as expected."

She folded her hands on her lap. "Ah, no. We decided to abort. I guess he's turned in all the paperwork, the report . . ."

"It's all in." Logan's strong voice sounded cold, very businesslike.

"I would have liked to have read it."

"I'm surprised you didn't," Edward said. "I'll put a copy on your desk. You should have done that yourself, Logan, or let her review it first."

He frowned at Tess. "I didn't know it was such a big deal. I summarized what happened. You do remember what happened, don't you?"

Why the animosity? She nodded. "Sure, I remember. It's okay, Edward."

"Why don't you take a look at it first, Tess, and make sure nothing was left out inadvertently?"

She appreciated Edward's attempt to get her input, but the scowl on Logan's face made her shake her head.

"I'm sure Logan got it all, never mind."

"I guess the question is, what now?"

"I've got a list of alternatives," Teresa said right away, having done some research to let Edward know that they hadn't given up.

They discussed her list. Both she and Logan were to spend the rest of the week on the phone, coming up with an alternative by the end of the week.

She went back to her desk feeling like a complete loser.

"What the hell was all that about?" Logan placed his hands on the edge of her desk and leaned across it. His mouth grim.

"What are you talking about?"

"Why were you questioning me in there?"

"I just thought we'd go over the report together before you turned it in, that's all, but like I said, if you took care of it, then okay, it's done."

He narrowed his eyes. "What's wrong, Teresa? What's up?"

She wanted to ask him the same question. Why was he so angry? But from the look on both Edward and Logan's faces when she walked in, she could guess. He'd taken the brunt of Edward's anger at their failure. She smiled. "I'm tired, that's all. I think I'll only work half a day today. Edward will understand, won't he?"

Logan straightened and shrugged. "I told him I'm taking a couple of days off. Gotta spend some time with Karen and the kids. Just tell Edward what you want and do it."

Teresa nodded. "Right."

Logan offered her a brief nod back. "See you around." He strolled to his desk.

See you around? After spending every minute together the past few weeks, eating with him, working, playing, dreaming, breathing Logan Wilde, he just walks away with "see you around?" That's it? Was it over between them so soon?

She turned on her computer, determined not to drive herself crazy thinking about Logan. About five minutes into her work, though, she couldn't help herself. She glanced his way and was immediately sorry. As always was the case, women swarmed his desk as he leaned back in his chair, hands tucked behind his head, smiling and chatting. She closed her eyes; the pain was too much. Returning her attention to the computer, she turned everything off, swung the bottom drawer out with more force than was necessary, yanked her purse out, and left work for the day. To hell with telling Edward, and to hell with Logan.

CHAPTER NINETEEN

If Teresa just ignored the phone, it would stop ringing. She snuggled deeper under the blankets. The phone rang for the fifth time. Why wasn't it going to voicemail? Eighth ring. Teresa sank her head into the feather pillow. Tenth ring. Damn! It had to be her sister. She hurled the covers off, flapped her sock-clad feet all the way to the living room, and picked up the cruel ringing beast out of her purse.

"Yes," her voice was croaky.

"Tess?"

"Logan?"

"Were you sleeping already?"

"I've been sleeping since I got home this afternoon. What do you want?" She sat on her couch, elbows on her knees and forehead on her free hand.

"Just to talk to you. I've gotten used it."

She wasn't sure how to respond to that. She sighed. "Me too."

"Can I come over?" His voice was soft and pleading.

She wanted him to, more than anything, she wanted to be in Logan's arms, if only to know that what they shared hadn't been just a fluke. "Why?"

"So we can talk, have some wine, hang out, have a good time."

And make love . . . but that was understood. Or was it? Sex, yes, but would he be making love to her? It wasn't fun anymore, not when she'd lost her heart and all she was to him was "a good time." "I'm too tired, Logan. I just want to go back to bed."

"Now I really want to come over."

She managed a breathy laugh. "Not tonight, okay?"

He laughed as well, then in a stronger tone, "I caught hell from Edward this morning. It kind of put me in a bad mood, sorry."

"It's okay."

"I feel strange being home again. Do you?"

"A little, kind of out of sorts. We probably need to sleep and get reoriented into the time zone."

"Maybe, but it's more than that. I feel like I don't belong in this cold, lonely apartment. I felt like a stranger at work today. I don't know . . . I feel like I need . . . ."

"What?"

"You, Tess."

She drew in a shaky breath. God, it felt good to hear him say that. She was glad she wasn't the only one feeling needy. "That's the sweetest thing you've ever said to me."

"Yeah, well . . . Will you come to dinner at my sister's tomorrow night? I'd like to introduce you to her."

Teresa smiled. This was a big step for Logan, and she knew it. "I'd love to."

"Yeah? Okay then. I guess I'll let you get some sleep. I'll pick you up tomorrow."

"I can't wait to see you."

"Teresa?" He sounded troubled.

"Yes?"

"I'm glad you stole half of my Patagonia account."

She laughed and lay back on her couch. "And I'm glad you stole half of *my* account."

He chuckled also. "Good night, sweetheart."

***

Logan slept miserably, waking up in the middle of the night with terrible shakes. He'd been dreaming of Teresa, then the dream switched to his parents. He hadn't dreamed of them in years. He leaped out of bed and shivered as he paced the room. He pulled a sweat top over his tank T-shirt and sat on the edge of the bed.

It wasn't the dream that bothered him, and he knew it; it was Teresa. He'd gotten too close to her, and that had never been his intention. He rubbed his face. No, everything would be fine. They were good friends, liked each other, enjoyed great sex, that was all. There was nothing to panic about. He crawled back into bed. Nothing to panic about.

***

"How was work today?" Logan asked as Teresa slid her shapely legs into the passenger side of his car.

She leaned across and gave him a peck. "I spent the day on the phone. I've contacted the top five industrial plants on my list. How was your day off?"

Logan gazed at her full red lips, not really caring to discuss work. He wanted more than a quick hello kiss. He cupped his fingers around the back of her neck and pulled her face forward. Slowly, he slid his mouth back and forth against hers. He could feel her lipstick coating his lips. She placed her right hand on his left shoulder and parted her lips, a sigh escaping. Her warm breath smelled minty fresh. Logan groaned. He wanted her, right now.

He pulled back and gazed at her lips again. The lipstick, once neatly outlining her lips, was now smeared all over. "You're dangerous, Lady."

She closed her eyes and leaned her forehead on his. "Are you going to kiss me or not?"

"I'm going to do more than that, Tess, but later." He eased her back into her seat and himself behind the steering wheel.

She took out a paper napkin from her purse, lowered her sun visor, and proceeded to clean her lips. She gracefully wiped the corners, dabbing here and there around the edges. He watched for a few moments, wishing she could leave it the way it was. She looked arousingly sensual with smeared lipstick. When she finished, she handed him the napkin and smiled. He smiled back, realizing he must look pretty funny with red lipstick all over *his* lips.

Unlike her careful clean-up job, Logan swiped the napkin a couple of times across his mouth. Then he started the car and concentrated on driving.

When they arrived at Karen's home, she welcomed Tess inside in what seemed to Logan, an overly enthusiastic display of hostessing. His little sister had acted surprised when he told her he'd invited Tess to dinner, but she'd smiled and agreed to buy steaks for Logan to barbecue.

They stood at the front door while Karen went on and on about how happy she was that Tess was joining them.

"How about you let us get farther in the house then?" he said.

Karen rolled her eyes. "Come in. The kids are playing in the backyard. We can sit out on the patio if you'd like."

"Sure." Tess followed Karen with a smile on her face.

Logan dumped charcoal into the barbecue, lit it, then went to tussle with the kids on the grass. Karen showed Tess her prized flower garden. Then they disappeared inside the house. He lay back on the grass to catch his breath. He watched the blue sky above begin to darken as night approached. Everything felt right again.

After dinner, Karen was putting the kids to sleep, and Logan pulled out the pictures he took on their trip to Argentina.

"I didn't see you take pictures."

"I took most of these at port stops."

"Oh, I like this one of the sea lion, it looks like a postcard."

Logan laughed. "He was a fat one."

"And these pictures of women on the beach?"

Logan grinned and ran his fingers through her hair. "I needed pictures of locals."

"I bet."

"Jealous?"

"Of course. I wish I looked like these women."

Logan slipped his arm around her shoulder and whispered in her ear, "Darling, you look better."

"Hey, should I go to bed too?" Karen interrupted as she waltzed back into the living room.

Teresa pushed him away. "Of course not, sorry."

Karen laughed. "Don't apologize—it's about time Logan started dating."

"We're not dating," he corrected Karen before she embarrassed Tess again.

Tess moved further away from him and began going through his pictures.

Karen shot him an annoyed look, then sat beside Tess. "He takes good pictures, doesn't he?"

"Mmm, yes, I like these skyline shots."

"He took those of the kids." Karen pointed to the framed photos on the wall unit.

Tess got up and went to examine the pictures. "They're terrific, Logan."

Logan leaned back and watched her. "Thanks."

"Are these your parents?"

Karen joined her. "Yeah, this was at our house where we grew up. Logan had just won a swim meet. See his medal?"

"You were so young."

"I was." Karen agreed. "This was a year before they died. I was only fourteen."

Tess shook her head. "Logan told me what happened. I'm so sorry."

Karen glanced back at him. "You told her?"

He nodded.

Tess frowned. "Was it a secret?"

Logan shook his head. "No, it's just that I don't usually talk about it. It's my fault they're dead."

"Logan." Karen gave him a hard stare.

"Relax, Karen, I'm not back to blaming myself, but facts are facts."

"What do you mean?" Tess looked from him to Karen.

"The fire started in my room, on my bed. I left the electric blanket on, like always, on an overloaded electrical outlet, even though Mom told me not to. It short-circuited and started a fire. And to make it worse, I left my cigarettes and lighter on the bed. The whole bed must have gone up like a firecracker."

Teresa's eyes were large and her mouth was open. "Oh my God, Logan. It was a terrible accident."

He nodded. "Yep, an accident, a damned accident. But at least I stopped smoking after that."

"That's not funny. Thank God you weren't in the bed."

"That's what I always said." Karen nodded.

Logan snorted. "If I had been in bed, I could have warned everyone to get out."

"No, Logan—." Karen began.

"Look." He bolted to his feet, not about to listen to a lecture about how it wasn't his fault. "I've gone over the 'what ifs' a million times. What if I had been there, what if you had, what if I'd have turned the damn blanket off, what if, what if. None of that matters, does it?"

Tess gave him a sympathetic look; her eyes were warm and loving, and he hated it. The last thing he wanted was a woman feeling sorry for him. He turned away from her. "That's life, I'm gonna get some water, excuse me."

He walked away, trying to act as if the past didn't still affect him. Teresa wanted to go after him so badly. She'd never seen Logan hurt like this before. He was always too busy showing everyone how happy he was.

"I wish someday he'd really believe that it wasn't his fault. I've told him a million times, but if I even talk about my parents, he begins to apologize because they're not here for me."

"It must be hard to live with that guilt," Teresa said.

"Are you ready to go?" Logan charged out of the kitchen.

"Anytime you are," Teresa went to the couch and picked up her purse.

He smiled. "Great, let's go. Karen, I'll be over tomorrow to take the kids to school."

"Okay, I'll have them ready. Nice to meet you, Tess."

He was quiet on the drive home, and Teresa didn't know what to say. "Thanks for dinner, you're a good cook."

"Sure, anytime."

She watched his profile and ached to touch him. "When are you coming back to work?"

"A couple of days."

She continued to stare at him, but he focused straight ahead on the road. "Karen's right, you do still blame yourself, don't you?"

He shrugged. "It's hard not to."

She placed a hand on his shoulder. It didn't seem possible for him to become more rigid, but he did. She pulled her hand away. "I guess you don't want to talk about it."

He glanced at her for just a second. "It was a long time ago, Tess. There isn't much to say."

But the tragedy had obviously created a huge scar. He hadn't overcome the guilt, especially if he couldn't even talk about his parents without thinking of the accident. "I don't believe that."

He frowned and drove faster. In fact, he drove so quickly that before she knew it, he pulled in front of her house. She released her death grip on the dashboard with a sigh of relief.

"I guess I'll see you at work," he said.

"Do you want to come in?"

His eyes took in her body almost insultingly, as if she were a piece of meat. "I'd like to, but . . . maybe some other night."

"Logan—"

"Good night, Tess."

"What are you doing?"

"I'm trying to drop you off."

"I mean, why are you acting so cold?"

He smiled. "I'm just tired, Tess. If I stayed, I wouldn't be much fun tonight."

"I don't care. I don't want to be with you only when it's fun."

He laughed. "Oh, sure, you want to be miserable with me."

"Yes, if you're miserable, I want to be miserable with you. I care about—"

"Don't! I'm not asking you to say anything stupid, so don't do it."

"Stupid? I don't feel stupid for caring about you."

He closed his eyes. "Get out, Tess. It was a good night. Let's leave it at that."

She didn't understand why he couldn't accept comfort. He'd revealed a painful part of his past, but now seemed to want to shut it and *her* out. "Oh, Logan." She reached across and touched his arm. "Come in with me. Let me hold you."

He took a deep breath, then turned the usual warm brown eyes to her, but this time she saw nothing, no feeling. "If you don't leave now, you're going to ruin our friendship, understand? I don't need complications. I want to go out and have a good time, and when it's no longer fun, then it's over."

She felt like he'd just dropped a bowl full of ice on her. She shivered. "I guess it's over." Her hands shook as she groped for the door handle. She found it and left his car with a heavy heart. Logan Wilde didn't love her. He couldn't love anyone; it was too complicated.

CHAPTER TWENTY

Monday's staff meeting moved quickly. After rehashing old news, watching slides on what was coming out in the next quarter, assigning new accounts, and filling everyone in on Teresa and Logan's problems in Argentina, everyone was excused except Teresa and Logan.

"What's the update on the wool suppliers, Tess?" Edward Reed leaned on his desk and crossed his arms.

"I've got five possibilities."

"Good. Where are they located."

"Two in Australia, three in Argentina."

"Perfect. Logan, you take Australia, Tess Argentina. Research them, then decide on one, maybe two, but come up with something soon. I need a good, quality supplier, and I need one immediately. I mean it. I don't want to see either one of you until you can present me with a signed contract." Then he sat behind his desk as a signal that he was finished with them both.

Tess lifted her notes off the table and hurried out. Logan caught up with her on the way to her desk.

"I guess we're stuck together on this account until we get it right," he said in a light teasing tone.

She glanced at him from the corner of her eyes. "It appears so."

He shot her a devilishly sexy smile. "Of course, working with you isn't painful at all anymore."

She slapped her papers on her desk and faced him, not returning the smile. Did he realize how hurt she was? Did he care? No, she realized, he didn't care. "Go research the Australian companies, Logan, and stay far away from me."

"Hey," he said, the corners of his lips drooping. "Ease up. I'm just joking around."

Her eyes stung. "You don't get it, do you, Logan? You . . . oh, forget it." There was no point wasting her breath on him. She started walking around him, but he gripped her upper arm.

"Look, I'm sorry about Friday night."

She narrowed her eyes as she stared at his frowning face. "Are you?"

"It was nothing personal."

"I know. I realize that now. Let my arm go, please, we're at work."

"Ah, Tess." His face darkened, and his eyes revealed deeply buried pain. "Don't do this."

"Don't do what?" Her voice cracked, so she stopped and took a deep breath. "Don't care about you, don't ask you for any kind of substance from our relationship? All right, you got it, Wilde."

He stared at her a little longer, then without a word, stalked away.

Later that day, when she came back from lunch, she found a check and a note from Logan on her desk. She stared at the note unbelievingly. It read, "For your parents." Although they'd talked about it and she'd agreed to borrow money from him, after their fight, his money felt like an even bigger brush-off. Her first impulse was to rip the check into a million pieces, but then she remembered the emerald earrings and that Logan offered things from his heart. She opened the top right drawer of her desk and placed the check under a stapler. She just couldn't cash it. Not anymore.

Their relationship remained tense in the days that followed. He took her list of proposed Australian suppliers and worked on them without consulting her. Their argument didn't seem to affect his work performance, or more accurately, lack of performance. He still breezed in and out of the office at will, joked and laughed with the others, and went on with his life as if Teresa had never existed.

She worked hard as usual, but the pain was eating her up a little more every day. How had she fallen in love with him? She should have known better. She'd seen how he was. For three long years, she'd seen how immature and irresponsible he was, yet she'd let herself be drawn in by his playboy personality. She had no one to blame but herself.

She made it to the end of the week with barely enough energy to go home and climb into bed.

Logan sat in the dark at his desk researching the two Australian sheep farms on the Internet. Friday night, and he was still working. What was wrong with him? He should have been out on a date, but he didn't feel like going out. He should be with the kids, but that didn't appeal to him either. He knew what he wanted . . . to see Teresa.

Out of all the women he knew, why her? She was trouble; she'd gotten into his blood, and he didn't want that. Yet, he did want it. He wanted to be with her, to look into her eyes and tell her stories, to let her tease him and make him laugh. He wanted to know everything about her. He wanted to apologize for pushing her away and beg her to forgive him.

He thrust himself out of his chair. That's just what he would do.

With all the pent-up rage inside him, he banged on her door.

She opened it with a bewildered look on her face.

"My God, I was ready to call the police until I saw it was you. Are you crazy?"

He charged inside her house. "You can stop walking around the office like a wounded animal, Tess. I'm not responsible for your hurt feelings."

Her eyes widened. "You came to my house at eleven thirty at night to tell me that?"

"I'm sick and tired of seeing you depressed. You're getting even skinnier, you know?"

She frowned, color coming to her cheeks. "Don't worry about me. You're right, you're not responsible for me."

"I just wanted to be friends, to have a good time."

Tears appeared in her eyes. "Well, did I give you a good time, Logan?" Her voice was low and heartbreakingly sad.

He turned away from her and sat on her sofa. He bowed his head. His forearms were on his knees. "When my parents died, I thought I'd die too. I couldn't help but blame myself. Shit, when I found out it started in my room, on my bed, I . . . ." He shook his head at the horrifying images: the charred house, all their belongings gone, all their memories ashes. "I acted like a fool for a while. Did dangerous, reckless things. Edward was my dad's best friend. He gave me the job even though he probably knew I'd screw up. I didn't, until now." Logan raised his head and looked at Teresa. "While I'd been feeling sorry for myself, my little sister hooked up with a loser and got pregnant. In a way that was my fault too."

"No," she whispered.

He nodded. "Yes. So, is that the kind of pain you want to share with me?"

Tears rolled down her face, and he felt terrible for causing them. He hated this bullshit. He wasn't into feeling sorry for himself, and he didn't want anyone else to either.

"I don't want to share your pain, Logan. I can't. I just want more than a few laughs and a bottle of wine. I want—"

"What do you want, Tess? A commitment? A confession of my undying love?"

More tears fell. She walked closer, then she knelt between his legs. "Yes."

His heart did a flip. She looked like an angel down on her knees, staring up at him with hopeful, watery eyes. He ran his hands down the sides of her head, wiped the tears with his thumbs, then leaned down and kissed the sweet lips he adored. "Were both here today, now, why worry about tomorrow?"

Her lips trembled. "Because not everyone will die on you, Logan."

He dropped his hands from her face. What was she talking about? His muscles on his face and back seemed to be tightening of their own accord. "I'm willing to carry on this affair as long as it lasts. That's all I can promise you. Anything different would be a lie."

"This affair. Is that all I am to you?"

"Tess—"

"Answer me. What do you feel for me, Logan?"

"I don't know. I like you, I'm attracted to you, I want you."

She looked disappointed. "That's just . . . not enough."

"I never promised you more, damn it. You agreed—"

"I know what I agreed to. But something happened between us, Logan. I felt it, and you did too, I know you did."

He eased back on the sofa. "Tess, I like you, that's no secret. And like I said, I want to keep seeing you, but you seem to want more. I'm not prepared—"

"It's all right. I'm sorry, I guess I'm just not capable of handling a nice, cold, uncomplicated affair, the way you are. My mistake."

He shook his head. This wasn't going well. "Look, what happened between us was—"

"Nothing happened, according to you. You think by living for today you're taking all life has to offer, but you're not. You're not even close. Just leave, Logan." She stood and hugged her arms around herself.

"Don't throw me out. You don't want to do that." He stood and placed his hands on her shoulders. If he touched her, held her, she'd soften toward him.

"What I want, you can't give me."

"Tess, honey, I need you." He squeezed his hands tighter on her shoulders.

She shook her head. "You're afraid to need anyone."

He let her go and rubbed his eyes with his knuckles; they stung. He shook his head and went to her door, standing there staring at the closed door. "I do need you, and you're right, it does scare me." He glanced back at her.

"Well then, there's nothing left to say." She came to him and grabbed the doorknob, pulling it open. "If you're afraid to need me, then you'll never let yourself really get close, will you?"

His vision blurred again. *Damn!* "Why can't we just keep our relationship light and enjoy each other's company the way we were, Tess?"

"Because I *love* you, and that's tearing me apart. Can't you see that?"

He felt like someone had sucked all the air out of his lungs. Yet, he wasn't surprised. He knew Tess wasn't the kind of woman he'd be able to have a cheap fling with, yet he'd pursued her anyway, because he'd wanted her. He was a selfish lowlife.

"I'm sorry, Tess. The last thing I wanted to do was hurt you. I didn't want this kind of involvement; believe me, it's too painful." He wanted to pull her into his arms, but he knew in order to do that, he had to reciprocate her words of love, and he couldn't do that. "I'm so sorry."

He left her house, afraid that he was making yet another mistake in his sorry life.

***

Teresa barely talked to him after that. They collaborated on the wool account. She said only what was necessary to get her point across. He'd never felt so worthless in all his life. It hurt that she wouldn't look him in the eye, that she was so proper and businesslike with him, just like she had been before they'd had that sensational trip together. He tried not to remember what it felt like to have her touch him, to be inside her, but he did remember, and he wished it could be like that again.

As they worked through lunch one day, he couldn't help himself. He laid a hand over hers. She froze in mid-sentence. "What are you doing?" She asked in a barely audible voice.

"I needed to touch you, Tess."

She stared at their joined hands. "Let this be the last time you ever do." She pulled hand free, got up, and left for lunch.

When she came back, he noticed her eyes were a little puffy and red-rimmed. His throat closed. He focused on the computer, where little penguins waddled around a black-and-white checker-board screen. This job, which was always so much fun, held no interest anymore. His life was a joke. He'd made it that by keeping everything light and people at a distance. Karen and the kids were the only things that mattered . . . and Tess mattered.

He'd better admit it before it was too late. She mattered to him. She was the kind of woman who came along only once. She'd given him herself openly and lovingly, even when he'd offered her nothing in return. She gave him her love, and he'd rejected it.

He made a fist and scoured his knuckles on the edge of the desk, creating little knocking sounds. He continued to turn his wrist over and over until his knuckles were red. But he felt no pain; all the hurt was bottled up in his heart. He glanced at Teresa's desk and saw her lift her purse and practically run out of the office.

He cursed. When his parents died, he promised himself he'd make the most out of his life. He wouldn't waste one second, because life was too short, too precious. And here he was throwing away the most wonderful woman he'd ever met. His parents would have loved Tess. *He* loved Tess.

Logan realized what he'd done. He hadn't made the most of his life at all. He'd spent all his time holding on to the guilt and not living the life he should have, a fulfilling life that included love. In his heart, he didn't believe he deserved that kind of happiness after the deaths he'd caused. But whether he deserved it or not, Tess did love him, and he wasn't going to lose her.

He got up and strolled to Edward's office.

"Glad you're here," Edward muttered.

"Yeah, why's that?"

"My wife's got some cookies for your sister and her kids."

Logan looked at the package on his desk, but his mind was not on cookies. "You said Tess was your first choice for the Patagonia account. Why did you send me?"

Edward's face lifted, and he studied Logan. "She's young, she's a woman, and I wanted her to be safe."

"So I was right. You wanted me to be her damn bodyguard?"

Edward frowned. "And apparently I sent the wrong guy."

"Go to hell, Edward."

"You're bright, Logan. You're management material. But you lack motivation. I figured if you spent some time with Tess, her determination might rub off on you."

"I'm good at what I do."

"Yes, you are, but do you want to be a buyer all your life?"

Logan frowned. "No, I don't."

Edward stood in front of Logan and gripped his shoulders. "Then what do you want?"

Logan looked into the eyes of the man who'd taken over his father's job. He'd been extraordinarily good to him and Karen. "I don't want to work for you anymore, Edward."

"What?" Edward looked shocked, hurt.

"I don't know what I want to do, I just know it's not this."

"Logan, you're upset and not thinking straight. Sit down, we can talk about this and—"

"No, I've made up my mind. And right now, I've got to go after Tess. She's what I want, Edward. She's all I want."

CHAPTER
TWENTY-ONE

Carla watered Teresa's porch plants, singing softly as she moved from one to the next.

The scent of damp earth filled the air as he approached. "Hi," he said, stepping up behind her.

She glanced over her shoulder, then straightened and faced him. "What do you want?" Carla's face was stone cold.

Logan swallowed. "I'm looking for Tess. She inside?"

Carla put the green watering can beside her feet. "She's not here."

"Oh, okay. I'll wait. How are you doing?"

"Look, pretty-boy, I told you not to mess with my sister."

He laughed. She was serious.

"I need to talk to her."

"She's not here. Go home." She picked up her watering can and turned away from him. She turned on the water hose and poured more water into the plastic can.

"I need to tell her I'm crazy about her. Whatever she told you—"

"That you're an immature, self-centered, unfeeling jerk who is in serious need of—"

"She said that?"

"I wasn't finished."

He nodded. "I got the point, you don't need to finish."

She shrugged. "It gets better."

Logan rubbed his forehead. "No, it doesn't, it gets worse." He sighed. "It gets a lot worse. But I want to make it right, Carla."

"Why are men so stupid?"

She didn't have to go that far. "Gives women something to feel good about once they fix us, I guess."

Carla smiled. "I guess." She began watering the flowers again. "Well, Mom wants to fix you all right. She's trying to make Theresita go see a *curandero*."

"A what?"

"A *curandero*, they cure you of spells cast on you, like spells of love."

Logan took a step closer to Carla and placed his hands on his hips. "Spells of l—, you mean your mother wants her to go to a witch doctor to cure her love for me?" He asked incredulously.

Carla chuckled. "Something like that."

"She's not there now, is she?" A crazy panic rose from the pit of his stomach and moved to his heart, which immediately began pumping at double speed.

Carla eyed him with an odd look in her eyes. "No, calm down. She's at my parents' restaurant. She's been working there nights, so I've been looking in on her plants and house. It's *El Horno* in Santa Monica. Look it up."

"She's been working at the restaurant?"

"Yeah, that way my parents don't have to spend money to hire someone else. They've had a money crunch, and Theresita has been trying to help them out. She gives them all her extra money, and now her extra time."

Logan stared at Carla. How wonderful to have a family that sticks together like that. Tess was so giving, so honorable, so responsible, so unlike him. He reached across and kissed Carla's bright red, plump cheek.

"Now, what did you do that for?" Carla placed a wet hand on her hip.

"Isn't it a Latin custom to kiss your sister-in-law goodbye when you leave?"

She laughed. "Sister-in-law? You've got high hopes."

"Yep." He smiled. "Thanks Carla."

***

Teresa looked like a Mexican flag. She had on a blazing red top with puffy short sleeves, which left her shoulders bare. Her skirt was green. And around her middle, she wore white fabric.

Logan asked to be seated in her section and watched her from behind his menu. Her hair was lifted up on her head, full of waves and curls. She looked so different, dressed like this, that he found it hard to reconcile the conservative, subdued Tess from work with this waitress as the same person.

She turned suddenly and stood at his table. He quickly lifted the menu in front of his face again.

"Ready to order?" she asked.

He slowly lowered the menu and watched her smile disappear.

"What are you doing here?"

Upbeat Mariachi music filled the restaurant. Sounds of people talking and laughing were all around them. But Logan had nothing to celebrate right now. He'd been a fool not to recognize what a wonderful woman she was earlier. "We need to talk, Tess."

"Now? Here?"

"I'll wait until you're off."

"No, go home—if you have something to talk to me about, do it at work on Monday."

"You won't even look at me at work."

Her eyes lowered, then she held out her hand. "I'll take that menu since you're not here to eat."

"Tess, honey—"

"Oh, please." She turned and headed toward the back of the restaurant.

Logan dropped the menu on the table and chased after her, weaving around festively decorated round tables. Teresa passed through double swinging doors into a kitchen, and he grabbed the white bow on her lower back to restrain her.

"Go away." She swung around and faced him.

"I will if you just agree to talk to me tonight. I could go wait at your house."

"No."

"Outside the restaurant, in the parking lot, anywhere."

"No," she shook her head.

"Tess," he placed his hands on her hips and closed the space between them. "I know we can work this out."

"Work what out? There's nothing between us."

"Bull."

A vice grip took his right shoulder and yanked him back. "Hey, what do you think you're doing to my daughter? Get the hell out of this kitchen."

"It's okay, Dad, he's a . . . co-worker."

"Co-worker?" The large Mexican man with bushy eyebrows and a heavy mustache turned a frowning stare to the left hand Logan still kept casually on Teresa's hip.

"My name's Logan Wilde. I'm in love with Tess."

"Who the hell is Tess?" her father growled.

"Oh God." Teresa shook her head. "Dad—"

Logan squeezed her hip tighter. "I am, Tess. I'm sorry I didn't say it before, but—"

"But you didn't. You had every opportunity, and you didn't. Leave, now—I don't want to talk to you anymore." She flew back out the double doors.

Logan started to go after her, but her father stood in front of him. Logan looked at the large man, then over his shoulder at the empty space where Teresa had been standing a second ago. "Look, Mr. Romero—"

"She told you to leave. The back door is over there."

"She doesn't want me to leave. She loves me."

"I certainly hope not," he snarled.

Logan glanced at the swinging doors again, then sighed and looked into her father's large brown eyes. They were the same as Teresa's. Logan gave him a crooked smile. "She does, and I love her."

"*Dios mio*, why me?" Mr. Romero looked at the ceiling as if he were praying with his eyes open.

"I love how beautiful she is. I love that she's kind and honest and hardworking and—"

"Enough."

"And I love that she's here, giving her time to help her family when she must be exhausted after working all day. I love that she can't cook, that she's stubborn, competitive . . . I love everything about her, Mr. Romero. I love your daughter."

Mr. Romero looked at Logan again, silently scrutinizing him.

"I believe you," he said and walked away, almost dejected.

Logan felt drained. Coming here had been a mistake. Tess deserved better than this. He loved her, and he had to tell her the right way. This wasn't it. He decided to take the back door after all.

***

It had been a long night, and her feet were killing her. She sat at the bar, her feet on the barstool beside her. Her father leaned across the bar and stared at her.

"I'll be back tomorrow night."

He nodded silently. "You're in love with that man."

"Dad—"

"Don't lie to me, *Tere*."

"I wasn't going to lie." She frowned.

"How can you be in love with someone I don't even know, someone you never even introduced me to?"

She rubbed her temples. "We went on a trip together for work, and it happened. You don't plan to fall in love; it just happens."

He gave a disgusted snort. "He's a lunatic."

She nodded, still pressing her fingertips to her temples. "I know."

Her father smiled, leaned across the bar and kissed her forehead. "He's in love with you, *mi'ja*. Coming in here and acting like a fool like that, he has to be."

Teresa smiled. "He always acts that way."

"*Dios mio.*" He shook his head and walked away.

***

Monday morning Teresa went to the office early. The sun was just starting to break through the heavy fog. Since it was so early, she was surprised to see Logan at his desk. His lanky body was stretched across his chair as he reclined into it. His clasped hands rested on his belly, and he seemed to be staring at empty space.

As soon as he noticed her, he lifted himself out of his chair and strolled over. They stood between his desk and hers, staring at each other.

"You're here early." Her voice echoed in the large office full of empty cubicles.

"I worked all weekend on the wool account. I've got the solution."

She'd finished researching and calling the three alternatives in Argentina, and she'd made her decision also. She held her purse over one shoulder, her laptop on the other shoulder, and her briefcase in one hand. She set everything down at her feet before facing him again. "I've made a choice myself. I've got the report for Edward."

"Let's see it."

She opened the snaps on her briefcase and handed him the report. He flipped through it and smiled. "It's perfect."

She released a breath she hadn't realized she'd been holding. "You agree?"

"That's what I'd decided too." He handed her back the report, his eyes never leaving her face.

She grabbed the report, but he didn't release it. She saw the serious look in his eyes and knew they had finished discussing the account. They had more important things to settle. She'd spent all weekend thinking about his declaration of love at the restaurant.

"I'm sorry, Tess."

"What are you sorry for?"

He sighed. He shook his head, and a crooked smile shaped his lips. "You want a list, huh? What can I say, Tess? I've been a fool." He moved forward, reached out an arm, and grazed her jawline with his index finger. His touch was so tender, and the look in his eyes so intimate, she had to suppress the desire to drop down on her knees and beg him to love her.

His hand descended from her face to her shoulder. His hand on her body was like a drug, sending her blood racing through her body, rejuvenating her. If only it had the same effect on her emotions. She seemed to be getting closer to tears with every passing second. "The time we spent together, was . . . ." He squeezed her shoulder. "I fell in love with you out there, Tess."

She drank in his warm brown eyes. She nodded. "I know, but I also know you consider it an inconvenience, and that you'd rather not love me. That hurts so much." Could she have any future with a man like that?

He let go of her shoulder. "Tess, I've wanted you since you came to work here three years ago. I knew the kind of woman you were, and I pursued you anyway, so the truth is, I did want to love you, and I do."

She tried to smile. "That's not what you wanted, Logan. You didn't want anything serious."

"You're right, I didn't. I haven't been living. Here I am, hiding out in a job I don't take seriously. I get involved in relationships I care nothing about. If I don't care about things and I lose them, then it won't hurt as much, I guess. That's pitiful, and it's not me. You helped me see that. That's why I'm handing Edward my two-week notice today."

"What?" *He's quitting?*

"I'm outta here, Tess."

She took a step closer to him. "You're leaving. Why?"

"Edward was good to me, and I'll always owe him. This job helped me out, but it's time I moved on."

"I can't even imagine coming to work every day and not seeing you."

He smiled, one of his wide, Logan smiles. "Maybe you can get used to seeing me after work?"

Everything was moving too fast. What exactly was he saying? "After work?"

"If you're willing to give me another chance, I'd like to start again, in the proper order: dating, engagement, marriage, children, you know, all that serious family stuff."

She smiled. "Marriage, children? I don't know about that. My dad hates you."

"Yeah, well, so did you at the beginning. I kind of grow on people, don't I?"

Yes, he did. She gave him a teasing smile. "It took me three years."

He gripped her upper shoulders and practically lifted her on her toes. He winced as if in pain. "I love you so much, Tess. I'll do whatever it takes to keep you, your dad, your whole family happy, if you'll just tell me you still want me."

The intensity of his eyes told her he was serious. Her heart raced, and emotion closed her throat. "I love—"

"Hey, I guess, I'm not the only one who decided to come in early." Edward's loud voice made them both shift back.

Logan smiled. "Hold that thought."

They followed Edward Reed into his office. Teresa placed the fifteen-page report on his desk. "This is who we should go with," she said.

Edward lifted an eyebrow. "The new wool supplier?"

Both Logan and Teresa nodded.

Edward flipped through the papers and frowned. "I don't understand?"

"*El Gaucho Estancia* was our first pick, and they continue to be the best. I'd like to fly back this week and close the deal," Teresa said.

Edward continued to stare at her with a dumbfounded look on his face. He leaned back in his chair and jiggled up and down. "If you couldn't close the deal the first time, what makes you think you'll be able to do it this time?"

"There was a misunderstanding, but I've talked with Juan Carlos Pennetti on the phone. He's willing to meet me at the administrative offices in Buenos Aires to renegotiate. I could close the deal in a week."

Edward smiled. "What about you, Logan?"

Logan handed him his resignation. "I'm gonna stay here and wrap things up while Tess closes the account in Argentina."

Edward sighed. "Are you sure about this?"

Logan nodded.

"Hell, let's do it then. Tess, pack your bags and leave. If you think you can close the account, go now."

Teresa looked at Logan.

He smiled. "Well, what are you waiting for? The faster you get out of here, the quicker you'll be back."

Even though Edward was watching, Teresa stretched up on her toes and kissed the first and only love of her life. "I love you, Logan Wilde," she whispered against his smiling lips.

***

Teresa left, went home, packed her suitcase, and drove to LAX. Juan Carlos had been skeptical when she called him on the phone, but he had immediately agreed to meet with her. He picked her up in Buenos Aires and drove her to her hotel. He was polite, kind, and accommodating.

The next day, they met at the business offices, which his mother ran. They spent the entire day discussing Juan Carlos' concerns. In the end, with compromises on both sides, they signed the agreement to become business associates.

Teresa knew she'd just closed the most profitable account of her career. She was happy, but the happiness didn't compare to the real joy in her heart that came from knowing Logan was home, waiting for her, and that he loved her.

TEN YEARS
LATER

Teresa welcomed Juan Carlos and his wife, Gloria, to the Penguin offices in Los Angeles. Penguin had grown to three times its original size in the last ten years. As one of the original founders, Edward retired four years ago, proud of what they'd accomplished. Teresa was immediately appointed the new president by the board of directors.

Excited to see her old friends, she embraced Gloria first, then Juan Carlos. "Sit down, please. We'll review some reports first, then head to our home for dinner. Logan is excited to serve you an Argentine *parrillada*. Humor him, please, even if it's not as good as yours. He's been planning it all week."

"I'm sure it will be delicious," Juan Carlos said. He and Logan had become long-distance friends. Once a year, Logan traveled to Argentina, where they fished, hunted, and bonded through outdoor activities.

"Food and a bed both sound like heaven. I hope you're not insulted if we turn in early tonight, Teresa," Gloria said. "That flight is so tiresome. I can never sleep."

"Your room is ready, and you can go right to bed and sleep for twenty-four hours if you want. But then, I'm getting you up. I've got tickets to Disneyland, and the kids can't wait to drag you onto every ride."

"Let's look at those reports, then," Juan Carlos said. "I'm hungry and tired too."

"Right, well, first your wool pools have worked amazingly well. The small producers you've gathered have added significantly to your yield, so thank you for that."

"Of course," he said, looking proud, and he should be. Penguin wasn't the only one to grow, but *El Gaucho Estancia* also expanded. Not their farm, per se, but Juan Carlos brilliantly connected with other producers and established centralized warehouses to store and process the wool that came in.

Penguin and El Gaucho Inc. had become such close partners that neither could exist without the other.

"Anyhow, I have all the figures there for you and new quarterly statements."

Juan Carlos looked it over, nodded, and stored it in his briefcase. "Perfect, Teresa. Gracias."

"How is your father, by the way?"

"Slower every day, but he's enjoying retirement. Since my mom passed, he's been more distant, you know? He forgets things and repeats others. The other day, he said we had to travel to Buenos Aires to see Mom."

"I'm so sorry," Teresa said. "I can't imagine losing the love of your life."

He reached for Gloria's hand. "Me neither."

They wrapped up their business, and Teresa drove them to their house in Santa Monica. After the kids reached school age, she and Logan moved out of Teresa's home and bought a larger house closer to her parents' house and restaurant. And they had extra rooms because someone was always visiting and spending the night, especially Logan's niece and nephew. Andy was fourteen with all the attitude of a teen boy. Karen had a hard time handling him, but Andy respected Logan, so Logan spent a lot of time guiding the boy. Stacy came less often now that she had a boyfriend and was getting ready for college.

As Teresa pulled into her driveway, she couldn't believe how lucky she was to have her family. She never would have imagined living such a blissful life with Logan when she started working at Penguin. Not a perfect life, because after all, he was Logan, which meant he was stubborn, and demanding, and always thought he was right, but he was also passionate, loyal, and deeply loving.

The smell of barbecued beef greeted them when they got out of the car. "That smells so good," she said. "Let me help you with your bags."

Teresa led them inside and placed the suitcases in the entry.

"Mommy," her six and eight-year-old girls chanted from the kitchen when she walked in. They ran to give her a hug. "Daddy said to make potato salad, so we're adding mayo to the potatoes," said Selene, the six-year-old.

Teresa kissed the girls and told them to say hello to their guests. "I will come look at your potato salad as soon as I show Juan Carlos and Gloria to their room."

The downstairs bedroom had its own bathroom and was perfect for guests. "Make yourselves comfortable, then come out to the backyard when you're ready. I'm going to see what kind of mess the kids are making in my kitchen and check with Logan on how the beef is coming along."

She found Logan in a cloud of smoke. Not that he wasn't an excellent griller—he was, but he had so much meat and ribs, and sausages on the grill that he seemed to be fighting constant flare-ups.

As she approached him, she admired his sexy bottom. Though he was still thin, he'd taken up so many outdoor activities and lifted weights at the gym regularly that he'd become more muscular, and his legs and bottom benefited most from his workouts. He turned his head, and a sleepy grin graced his face. "You are a sight for sore eyes, and I do mean sore eyes."

She smiled. "How's it coming along?"

"Almost done. Thank God." He stepped away from the grill and wrapped a hot arm around her waist. "I want to ask you about our guests, but first kiss me."

Teresa brushed her lips against his, deepening the kiss as he pulled her closer. You're going to need a shower," she said, as she pulled back.

"I'll let you give me one after dinner, but only if you take your time and promise to scrub every inch of me, rubbing those beautiful hands back and forth many times on the hardest body parts you find."

"You are a dirty man."

"I am." He chuckled and slapped her backside and returned to the grill. "And you love it."

Juan Carlos and Gloria came through the sliding glass doors, having changed into shorts and t-shirts. They looked tired, but much more relaxed and very Californian.

"Hey," Logan said, shaking hands with Juan Carlos and slapping him on his upper arm. "Looking good, my man. Chasing after those sheep is keeping you strong." He turned to Gloria and kissed her on the cheek. "And you get more beautiful every time I see you."

"Hands off my wife." Juan Carlos teased.

"Don't get jealous. I'm married to a Goddess. But you'd better watch her because other men are going to try to steal her from you, JC."

Gloria giggled, but then she said, "Don't say that. He's already overly protective and unbearably jealous."

"Because I love you, querida." Juan Carlos caressed Gloria's back.

They sat at the table under the back porch trellis as Logan took the sizzling meat off the grill and placed it on a platter. Teresa ran inside to see what the girls were doing, and to her pleasant surprise, they had prepared a beautiful potato salad with no mess.

"I made it just like *abuela* taught me," Ella said.

"Just like abuela taught *us*," Selene countered. "It has potatoes, and carrots, and peas, and relish, and—"

"She knows what the damned potato salad has. Her mother made it for her when she was a kid, remember?"

"Hey, Ella. We don't talk like that. Where did you learn that word?"

She shrugged. "Which one? Potato?"

Teresa raised an eyebrow. That smart mouth of hers constantly got her into trouble.

"Andy says damned all the time, and Daddy doesn't tell him not to."

Ella was eight, going on fourteen, just like the cousin she idolized.

"Well, you've said it for the last time. I'll talk to Daddy and Andy. Now, thank you for making the salad. It looks amazing. Both of you go to the backyard for dinner. I'll take the salad out."

But Selene jumped on Teresa. Her little monkey. Teresa picked her up and kissed her as her child wrapped her arms and legs around her. "How was kindergarten today?" When she started school, she cried every day for two months, not wanting to go to school, but lately, she'd decided it was kind of fun to have her own friends away from her domineering sister.

Selene shrugged. "Alex was going to be my boyfriend, but he stole my blue crayon, so now I don't like him anymore."

"You really can't trust boys who steal your crayons. I think you made a good decision to break it off with him." Teresa walked toward the backyard with Selene in her arms.

"Aside from that, did you have a good day?"

"No, because Stephanie has a little brother, and I don't, and she said I never will. Can I have a baby brother, Mommy?"

"I don't think so, baby."

"Please."

"I'll think about it." Teresa gave her another kiss and put her down. "Go find a place at the table to sit. I'll be right there." In the kitchen, she picked up the potato salad and a green salad Logan must have made earlier and carried them outside.

They ate and enjoyed a bottle of wine, catching up on farm life in Argentina. Juan Carlos and Gloria had only been married three years and didn't have kids yet, but they were trying.

After dinner, they all went inside to drink some coffee and tea. Logan broke out a sinfully decadent cheesecake drizzled with raspberry sauce that he probably picked up at the Cheesecake Factory.

"Hey, are these your pictures?" Juan Carlos pointed to the landscape photos that graced their walls. Logan had pursued photography, work he was passionate about. Every time he went to Argentina, he took hundreds of photographs of the amazing natural scenery: glaciers, sea life, pristine oceans, the Iguazu Falls. But, he also took pictures in America, selling them to magazines, entering them in contests, and displaying them in museums. When he wasn't traveling, he taught photography classes as therapy at organizations that helped children deal with traumatic events. He told his story about losing his parents in a fire. Soldiers dealing with PTSD, children who had suffered unspeakable traumas, from accidents to violent crimes, listened to him and lost themselves in art. He was a fabulous speaker and instructor. Students loved him, so he was invited back again and again.

"These are amazing. You have an eye for bringing out the motion in the motionless," Gloria said.

"Thank you," Logan gazed at his work, the ones Teresa loved the most and wouldn't let him sell. He dropped his hands in his pockets. "My favorite is that one, The Cave of the Painted Hands, from your neck of the woods. It looks like the hands are moving, depending on where you're standing.

"It does," Juan Carlos agreed. "Thank God you have a talent for taking pictures, because you were a shitty salesman."

"I was not," Logan said.

"Trust me, you were. And you're a worse fisherman."

"Now, those are fighting words, my friend. We're going to go fishing while you're here, and I bet I catch more fish than you do."

"That's a bet," Juan Carlos said.

***

Logan waited in bed while Teresa put the girls to bed. She worked such long hours that she didn't get to spend enough time with them. He was the one who took them to school, picked them up, helped them with homework, cooked, and he didn't mind at all. But Tess insisted on putting them to bed and making them breakfast in the morning. She was incredible. Always had been. She could run circles around him.

When she returned, she asked, "Ready for that shower?" She released her hair from a bun, and it flowed in waves onto her shoulders.

Sliding off the bed, he was already imagining how much he was going to enjoy this shower. He reached for her generous hips. "Let's get dirtier first."

"No, you smell like chorizos. Burnt chorizos."

"That's because I slaved over that grill to cook your meat just the way you like it." Logan nibbled on the side of her neck.

"You do know exactly how I like my meat, don't you?"

"You know it, Tessa baby."

She reached into his sweatpants, and immediately his body reacted, springing to life.

"Do you know what Selene asked me for?"

"Not a dog again." Dropping his head on her shoulders, he focused on what she was doing, trying to put his daughter out of his mind.

"Nope," she caressed him until he moaned. "A baby brother."

Logan lifted his head. "Really? I hope you told her she had a better chance of getting a dog. Or a penguin. She asked me to bring her back a penguin from Argentina."

"I think we should consider it," Teresa said, her hands sliding his sweats down his legs as she went down on her knees, looking up at him full of naïveté and heat. How did she manage that?

He stepped out of his sweats and boxers. "Consider what? Another baby? And don't look at me like that."

"Like what?" she said innocently. "Like I want to run tongue and lips all over you?"

"On second thought, look at me like that all you want. But do that in the shower." He pulled her up to her feet and helped her strip.

"One more baby would be nice."

"No."

"A baby boy." She sighed. "Wouldn't you want a son?"

"No more kids."

"Why not?" Now she sounded annoyed.

"Because I'm done with kids. I helped raise Karen's kids. I'm raising ours."

"*You're* raising ours? What does that mean?"

"Don't get mad, Tess. Come on. You work such long hours. The bulk of their care falls on me, and you know it."

Her face flushed, and it wasn't because she was turned on. He walked behind her and covered her breasts with his hands, then pressed his lips to her neck. Pressing his hips against her bottom, he closed his eyes. How did she get hotter each year?

"Mm, please. Just one more."

"Shh. Stop talking. We're going to go into that shower. You're going to show me how much you adore me."

"Yes?"

"And I'm going to carry you back to this bed and prove to you that you have everything you need to be happy."

She turned in his arms. "I know that. I'm crazy happy."

Logan gazed into her eyes. "Me too. Life is perfect. We're not missing anything, Tess. You don't need another baby."

"A little boy with your eyes would be so cute."

He led her toward the bathroom, where she went willingly. She lathered his body with soap, she kissed him, she washed away all of the day's worries, just like she'd done for the last ten years. She'd bathed him with love and made him a new man. No matter what he wanted: sex, a comfortable home, sex, exotic trips away, more sex, she gave it to him with all her heart. She lived her life to make him happy, and that was the truth.

If she wanted another baby, who was he to deny her? Shit, he'd take care of ten kids if Tess wanted them. He carried her bed after the water turned cold and made furious, passionate love to her until she bit her lip to keep from crying out his name.

They lay in each other's arms in the blissful exhaustion of lovemaking. He slowly caressed her belly. "Can we call him Matthew?"

Teresa angled her head. She was almost asleep. "Who?"

"Our baby boy. Matthew, after my father."

She rolled on her side, and her hand cupped Logan's face. "Really? You'll have another baby? You mean it?"

"Tess, I'll do anything for you. Anything that makes you happy. But make sure it's a boy, okay?"

She smiled a soft, sleepy smile. "How did I get so lucky to find you?"

"You found me. You loved me. You changed me. And now I'm forever yours. You're stuck with me, woman."

Tears filled her eyes, and she wrapped her arms around Logan. "I have everything I need. I don't need another baby. But thank you."

Logan breathed a sigh of relief and held his wife.

"Two beautiful girls." She eased back and kissed his lips. "And my first and only love. How could I ask for more?"

"You can ask, darling, and I'll give you whatever is in my power to give you." Logan held her as she fell asleep in his arms. As he drifted off to sleep, he remembered her walking into the offices of Penguin, where he was the peacock that all women wanted. She wore the ugliest business suit and looked completely uptight. But he'd seen the passion, the ambition, and the challenge. Tiger Tess. He'd arrogantly told himself that she'd be his. After all, women loved him. If he wanted her, he'd have her. But he'd been wrong. It happened the other way around. Logan had become hers. She'd conquered him. Stole his account, his job, and most importantly, his heart. She had him wrapped around her little finger, and he was the happiest man alive.

THE END

Here is a special advanced preview of:

Built to Win

by Lara Rios

On Sale: January 2026

CHAPTER ONE

J uly

Multicolored race cars circled the small track. Fire engine red.
Metallic green. Yellows. Blues. Some fast. Some trailing behind. They
created a dizzying blur of color in the scorching heat typical of the
Bakersfield desert. Occasionally, a car pulled off to the side or onto the
middle of the track, and a driver popped out of the window.

Gabriela Alende approached the chain-link fence separating the
empty public seating from the racetrack where the drivers practiced
for that evening's race. She placed her forehead on the chain-link fence,
closing her eyes. She longed to block out the painful memories that
resurfaced with every passing car. But even with her eyes closed, the
revving engines and acrid smell of gasoline only reminded her of the
awkward, lonely years of her adolescence that she had desperately tried
to erase from her mind.

She opened her eyes and stared absently at the cars tearing across the
track as dust from the surrounding area drifted in the air. Just the sight
caused a tightness in her throat, suffocating her. What kind of solace
had her father gotten from these loud, dirty tracks? Gabriela drew a
deep breath and eased back a wisp of light brown hair that had worked
loose from her orderly French braid.

As she turned, her eyes traced a path over the empty
stands—bleachers stretched out in neat rows, the metal seats glint-

ing in the harsh desert sunlight. By tonight, families would occupy almost every seat, and perhaps this was the one thing she recalled with fondness. The lively race crowd was different from fans of other sports. Maybe because so many kids attended with their parents and ran around waving flags. The atmosphere was comparable to that of a carnival more than a sporting event.

The fun actually began hours before the race started. Only after buying food and memorabilia of their favorite car and driver at the various vendor trailers would the fans sit and enjoy the race. How many times had she witnessed the same scene? The last time had been three years ago when she and her father had parted ways. She shook her head. In some ways, it felt like just yesterday.

"Track's not open yet." A gruff female voice called. "Can I help you?"

Gabriela squinted past the bright sunlight. She drew a second steadying breath to mentally bring herself back to the present, and she regretted it instantly. The smell of exhaust made her nauseous. "I'm Gabriela Alende. I'm—."

"I know who you are." The tall, athletic woman stopped in front of her. "I'm sorry about your father."

Gabriela nodded. For the last two weeks, she'd had to endure endless phone calls and visits from people who were sorry. She was sick of hearing those words. What exactly were they sorry about? All she wanted was to get past her father's death and move on with her life. "I received the beautiful bouquet from the speedway with all your condolences. Thank you."

"I'm Billie, by the way, the announcer." She held out her hand.

She shook Billie's hand.

"So, what brings you here?" Her eyes strayed to Gabriela's clothes as she released her hand.

Gabriela wore a lavender sundress and two-piece platform sandals with two-inch heels, a fashion better suited for a stroll through a museum. She obviously wasn't dressed for a day at the track. Maybe this was the last way she could rebel against her father. Or perhaps merely a way to deny what she was about to face.

"My dad's car," she said.

"Yep, number 58."

"I'd like to speak with the driver, Cruz Ortega if he's here."

"Should be in the pits getting ready for tonight." Billie looked at the track. "He's not out practicing yet."

"Can I get into the pits on my own?"

"Come on, I'll take you. You're not pulling the car from the circuit, are you?" Billie's slender frame walked gracefully in front of Gabriela, leading her toward the pit area. She wore a black racing jumpsuit with the speedway's red logo emblazoned on the back, and her long hair was pulled into a tight ponytail.

The ground beneath their feet was hard and uneven, the surface littered with crumbs of tire rubber and bits of debris from the track. Gabriela wasn't sure what she was going to do. Of all the crazy things for her father to leave her—a race car. "I need to talk with Mr. Ortega. He probably knows the car better than anyone."

Billie nodded. "You're right there."

She followed Billie behind the track, where some cars were in various states of being repaired while others were parked and ready for tonight's race.

They stopped beside a shiny, royal blue Ford Taurus with the white number 58 painted on the side. The hood was up. Three men with grease on their hands were pulling things out of the engine.

"Don't change the spark plugs until after the first race," said the one bent over the engine.

"Cruz." Billie tapped the man's solid arm.

Cruz looked over his shoulder, keeping one arm in the car. Gabriela got her first glimpse in years of Cruz's rugged heart-stopping good looks. Dark, thick eyebrows cast a shadow over his eyes; sultry, pink lips; short, wind-tossed black hair. He straightened. "Hey, Billie." His eyes flickered over Gabriela, and he frowned. "What's up?"

"You've got a visitor."

He glanced at Gabriela again. "What's she want?" he asked Billie.

Why was he acting as if she weren't standing right behind him? Gabriela stepped closer. "I need to speak with you."

His frown remained, his forehead full of creases, and his eyebrows drawn together. "All right. Speak."

Gabriela looked at the others staring at her. Somehow, she'd pictured being able to discuss her business somewhere different. How could they hold such a personal conversation with engines revving and roaring to life—with so many people around? "It concerns this car."

"I figured it did, Miss Alende."

So, he remembered her. She felt a spark of pleasure for the first time since walking onto the speedway grounds. "The car is my responsibility now that my father's gone."

"Yeah," he said. "Guess I expected he'd be leaving it to you."

She inhaled, trying to read his cold gaze. "Well, I didn't. It's the last thing I expected him to leave me." Especially since he knew how much she hated the track.

Cruz crossed his arms and leaned his backside against the car door. He'd matured and filled out. She noticed how the fabric of his shirt stretched tight around the thick bands that formed his upper arms and how his torso narrowed to sexy, slender hips.

"Beggars can't be choosers," he said after staring at her for several moments. "An American saying, isn't it?"

She wasn't sure what he meant by that, but she didn't like his attitude. "I need to figure out what to do with this car."

"Yes, you do."

"I hoped you might be able to help me."

"How?"

Gabriela swallowed. "I don't know much about racing."

"No." He uncrossed his arms and placed his hands on the car behind him, repositioning his hips slightly, distracting Gabriela. "You didn't exactly hang out at the track when your father was alive."

Oh, yes, she had more than she cared to remember. She'd spent every weekend for twelve years trapped at these speedways while her father neglected her. The moment she turned eighteen, she went away to college to get as far away from her father and the racetrack as she could. Cruz probably didn't remember, and she wasn't here to argue with the driver. Let him believe what he wanted. "Which is why I need your opinion on—."

"My opinion?" He laughed. "How about a fact? This was a game to your father, but it helps pay my bills. Opinions aren't important here," he said.

"I understand."

"So now what? You tell me."

"Well, okay, we keep racing, I suppose. I'll learn whatever I have to to keep the car on the track."

He raised an eyebrow. "You mean you're going to keep running the car?"

"Yes." Was she? She wasn't sure what she wanted to do; how could she sound so decisive? Maybe because he seemed to be challenging her, and she could never resist a challenge.

He smiled. "Great. So, I can still count on a paycheck." He pushed off the car and stood.

"Mr. Ortega—."

"Cruz."

"About paying you . . .." Gabriela shifted on her feet, uncomfortable, unsure how to tell him.

"What about it?"

"Well, it might be a little difficult at first. My father left me this car but nothing else."

Cruz's eyes widened. "Nothing? What do you mean by nothing? Your father's business, properties, and investments are worth millions."

"Nothing. This car is my entire inheritance."

Cruz lifted his chin as if understanding. "He left you a hundred-thousand-dollar car without the means to maintain it." He shook his head. "That's funny."

"I'm glad you think so." She adjusted her purse and straightened her back. "Look, what I'm trying to say is I have no extra money, just the car."

The frown reappeared. "What about maintaining the car, traveling, my salary? How do you intend to pay for those things?"

"I don't know. It can come from what we earn, I suppose."

Cruz glanced at Billie, then behind him at the guys listening with interest. He took Gabriela's arm. "Let's go for a walk."

They left the pits together, walking side by side until he led her beneath the bleacher stands. The moment they stopped and faced each other, the contrast between them was striking. She stood before him in a clean dress with not a wrinkle or stain in sight. Meanwhile, Cruz's T-shirt was torn at the collar, and smudges of grease covered his chest as if he had wiped his hands on the fabric. This morning, she had applied a delicate lavender lotion to her fair arms and legs after her shower. In contrast, his face was darkened by car exhaust and glistening with sweat. He carried the scent of grease and cedar aftershave. But Gabriela suspected that their differences ran much deeper than just appearance or artificial scents.

"A racing team costs money," he said.

"I know—."

"And you don't have any?"

"No, but—."

"Then you'd better forget about racing the car." He lifted a foot and placed it on an iron bar, and leaned his back on a support beam, looking at ease with himself and his surroundings.

"But, you'll make money, won't you? In fact, I'm counting on it. If you win a few races, we'll have enough to maintain the car, and I can pay my personal bills."

He shook his head. "Doesn't work that way."

"Why not?"

"Just doesn't. If you aren't prepared to dump lots of money to keep the car running, this is our last race."

Gabriela didn't have a penny, didn't he understand? "Cruz, I'm not going to spend money on this car? I want it to make me money."

"It won't."

She pressed her fingertips to her forehead, where her freshly mani-cured nails scratched her skin lightly. Her temples began to throb. All those years she spent attending races, and she'd never bothered to learn the business or what her father actually did to run his car.

She assumed that as the owner, her father sat back, watched the races, and cashed a big check at the end of each night. It wouldn't make sense for him to pay for a car that was draining him financially. Not only didn't it make sense, it wasn't in his nature. Carlos Alende never in his life did something that lost him money. Obviously, Cruz didn't know what he was talking about. "If you keep racing and win, you'll make money, right?" she asked.

Cruz laughed. "Oh, I can, and with that, you'd be lucky to buy the guys a beer at the end of the night and refuel the car."

"You're telling me there's no profit?"

He stood upright and came closer to her. "I'm telling you, the expenses are tremendous. I'm also telling you that if you expect that car to win many races, you're out of your mind."

"But why can't it? Aren't you a good driver?"

This time, he frowned. "The point is," his voice turned cold. "The car is old. It constantly needs replacement parts. It's not a winner; it's a racer."

Gabriela sighed heavily. "Replacement parts?"

"Engines, tires, and that's just for starters."

"Well, the car must make more than enough to cover those kinds of expenses."

He rolled his eyes, looking upwards, then swept his hand across his sweat-drenched brow and into his scalp, moistening his coal-black hair. With obvious irritation and fading patience, he faced her anew. "This is the Southwest Series. We don't make money, Miss Alende; it's just fun."

"No, this is a business. I've driven three hours in the desert heat to get here, and all I want to hear is that you'll keep racing the car and win so we can use the prize money to keep us all from starving."

He shook his head. "Have you heard anything I've said in the past ten minutes?"

"You don't understand. I don't have anything else to fall back on. This is it." She swallowed the lump in her throat. The past few weeks were beginning to take their toll on her. Reality was setting in—she was broke. Worse than broke, she had nothing now, no one. She needed just one person on her side.

His eyes narrowed, and he stared hard and cold at her. "Am I supposed to feel sorry for you, Gabriela?"

"No, I–."

"You asked for my opinion. Here it is. Sell the car, take whatever money you get, and run." He gave her body an intimate scanning. "This is positively not your thing, Querida." He turned and walked away, ending their discussion without a care about what would happen to her.

"Cruz, wait." Gabriela reached for his arm, desperate to make him understand. At twenty-four years old, she'd never worked a day in her life, but she was willing to. She'd spent the last six years in college as an art major. She supported herself with a few thousand dollars her father automatically deposited into her bank account every month.

But all that was gone. She had used the money to live on, travel, and buy art, always figuring she was young and had plenty of time to decide on a career and find a job. Now, she wished she had been more responsible. But she never dreamed her father would die so young and give his entire estate away to charity. If this car didn't make money for her, she didn't know how she'd survive.

Cruz looked from her hand on his arm to her face. "What?"

"As long as I own that car, and you're under contact to drive it, you have to do what I tell you."

His eyes hooded, and the color of his face darkened. He turned completely around and faced her, looking like a thundercloud hovering above her. "Gabriela, you're a young woman, a child still. You are not going to hang around a track full of men, and you are definitely not going to tell me what to do. Understand?"

She stiffened, lifting her face to meet his eyes, unwilling to let him intimidate her. Who was he calling a child? "I will be at every race from now on, Cruz. You'd better get used to it."

He moved closer. One arm shot out, and he gripped one of the bleacher's criss-cross supports over her head. She took a step back, but her eyes remained locked on him as she stared at his handsome face.

"You think I don't remember who you are, Gabriela? Because I do."

What did he mean by that?

"You might not remember me," he continued.

"Of course, I remember you." He was a skinny kid when her father hired him seven years ago, not much older than she was. Sweet. He didn't speak much English.

"Do you?" His voice dripped with disdain, challenging her. "You remember when your dad walked out of the office the day he hired me, and that you kissed me? Remember that?"

"No." But she did. She'd sat in his office, off to the corner drawing, pretending she wasn't paying attention. But couldn't keep her eyes off Cruz. He was beautiful and seemed so eager to get hired and to please her father.

Cruz smiled cruelly. "No, huh? Why would you remember? You were just having a little fun with one of your father's lowly drivers. Isn't that right?"

She could only stare into his challenging black eyes. At seventeen, she'd thought Cruz was the sexiest, most masculine man she'd ever seen. Just arrived from Mexico, he was different, exotic, tempting. But it was the innocence in his eyes that had captured her. She didn't see any of that anymore.

He moved closer; his face was just above hers. Their lips almost touched. She saw the film of moisture on his temples and brow, smelled his aftershave, and felt the heat from his body.

"Kiss me again," he said.

She swallowed, gazed at his lips, then at his stony eyes. "Step back," she said.

"Or?"

She narrowed her gaze, wondering what it would feel like to connect her knee with his groin.

Then, all of a sudden, he released his grip on the bleacher above her head but didn't step back. He lowered his head, his lips practically touching hers. "Aren't you going to stop me?" He whispered.

"I'm waiting to see what kind of asshole you've become."

He chuckled, then eased back.

She sighed, relieved. Already, she was envisioning his hard kiss, feeling him parting her mouth with his own sensual, full lips, and inserting his tongue. He left her with the longing for his taste. Damn him.

"I'll tell you again, this is no place for a beautiful, young, pampered girl like you. I'm the closest you're going to find to a gentleman here. Goodbye, Gabriela."

She watched him retreat, too stunned to react. She touched her lips as if he'd actually pressed his to hers. Had she heard him correctly? Had he said she was beautiful? She closed her eyes and tried to clear her mind. What did it matter if he thought she was attractive? The only thing she needed from him was for him to drive the car well, win races, and make money. But he seemed so sincere when he said that wouldn't happen.

She turned and headed to her car. She wasn't angry at Cruz. He made it clear that if she paid him, he'd keep driving. Her normal life had suddenly turned upside down. She was afraid, anxious, desperate . . . not angry. Above all, she was disappointed that the race car would not be the save-all money-maker she had expected it to be. What would she do now?

##

Cruz returned to the car and reached for his gloves in the toolbox.

"What did she say?" Danny asked.

He slid each hand into a glove and squeezed his fingers open and shut. He shouldn't have gotten so close to her, damn him. "Nothing."

"What do you mean nothing? Is she still going to race the car?"

Danny was young and energetic and passionate about cars, but he was also a pain in the rear at times. Cruz shrugged and moved past Danny, trying to remember what he'd been doing under the hood.

Danny leaned on the car beside Cruz. "Man, she's hot. I mean, if you can get past that miss hotshot attitude. Did you check out her–?"

Cruz straightened and hit his head on the inside of the hood. "Shit," he yelled. "Don't you have anything to do?"

Danny gave him an innocent look. "You're in a lousy mood."

"I'm racing today, in case you've forgotten, and I'd like the car to run. Do you mind?"

"All right, all right." Danny went around the car to finish his work.

Cruz tried not to think of Gabriela as he labored with the engine but found it impossible. After seeing her again, practically touching her, imagining her soft lips against his, his mind and body wanted nothing more than to remember.

He'd seen Gabriela maybe a dozen times in the past seven years, usually arguing with her old man. As the years went by and she'd changed from an immature seventeen-year-old to a woman in her twenties, he'd often daydreamed about kissing her again. In his imagination, it certainly never happened under a bleacher, with him sweating like a pig.

He'd always pictured her smiling, inviting him to kiss her, then to undress her, begging him to make love to her. He pushed away from the engine and yanked off his gloves.

"What's the problem, Cruz?" Danny wiped his brow and drew a grease stain on his forehead.

Why was he doing this to himself? Gabriela Alende was not the kind of woman he'd ever want. She wasn't nurturing or compassionate. Her interests and tastes were completely different from his. She dressed in clothes he imagined were so expensive, he couldn't afford them even if he spent his entire salary. Besides, he knew she was a cold, heartless bitch.

All she did was sponge money off her dad. A man Cruz would have walked through fire to please. But not Gabriela. The only thing she was close to was his wallet. "I guess that Alende chick got to me more than I thought."

Danny shook his head and laughed. "Heard she can do that. Yep, heard some really wild stories about her and the old man."

Cruz frowned. And they were all true. He still didn't understand why she didn't adore Carlos Alende as much as he had.

"Heard she flirted with the drivers, conned them out of beer, drove the old man crazy," Danny continued. "Did you know her then?"

Cruz shook his head and thought about the kiss she'd given him years ago. She'd done more than flirt, but he wasn't about to tell Danny and add to the gossip.

"I've got a headache," Cruz moaned. The back of his head was throbbing. "I'm going to get something cold to drink, okay?"

"Hey, relax, Cruz. I'll finish this, and Flip will be back soon. He went to buy us some burgers."

Cruz nodded. As he strolled away, he lit a cigarette. He blew out a puff from the side of his mouth, relaxing. Between his late-night racing schedule, janitorial work, and morning college classes, he was physically drained. He couldn't wait for the race season to be over so he could rest. He'd be out of the extra pay, but at least he'd catch up on his sleep. Of course, with Gabriela Alende being the new owner, he would probably be out of a racing job soon, anyway.

He missed Carlos Alende already. The pep talks he would give him, the pats on the shoulder . . . a man who understood hard work and loyalty, a man Cruz had admired like no other. That was precisely why Cruz would never be able to comprehend the distance between Gabriela and Carlos Alende. Didn't the woman realize what a treasure her father had been? Didn't family mean anything to her?

Cruz was close to his parents. He never would have disrespected them the way she did, Mr. Alende. In Mexico, Cruz helped his father at the auto shop every night. After going to school all day, he would put in another five or six hours working on cars so that his father wouldn't have to hire a helper. He'd missed out on some of his childhood and teenage years, but he didn't mind because he was making life easier for his father. He would go out of his way to please both his parents.

Gabriela and Mr. Alende didn't have that kind of relationship. Even at his funeral, she stood with no emotion on her face during the service. Immediately afterward, she walked away without listening to or acknowledging anyone's condolences.

What kind of woman didn't cry at her father's funeral?

He reached the concession stand, which was not yet open, but the girls always let him buy something before the race. He peeked inside the booth. "Hey, beautiful. Sure could use a large coke."

The cute eighteen-year old bent over, getting paper cups from a plastic bag, lifted her head, and smiled. "One soda coming right up." She filled a large cup, placed a lid on it, and handed it to him.

He gave her five dollars and winked. "Gabbyas. Keep the change."

She didn't speak Spanish but seemed to like to practice with him. "Muy gusto."

Cruz laughed. "Mucho gusto. Although, what I think you mean is de nada."

She shrugged sheepishly. Her mother walked in then. She and her three daughters ran the booth. "Still trying to pick up on my daughter, Cruz?"

He smiled. "Naw, just buying a Coke. Your girls are too smart to get involved with a guy like me."

She smiled and hustled around the grill, setting frozen hamburger patties at equal distance from each other. "If they were a little older, or I was a little younger, we'd snatch you up in a heartbeat, and you know it."

Cruz laughed and turned away. He was starting to feel better. He didn't know why he let someone like Gabriela Alende get under his skin. Just because the car now belonged to her didn't mean his life had to change. His driving record was pretty good. If things didn't work out with her, he could find another team to drive for and keep that badly needed extra income.

Of course, keeping the woman out of his thoughts would not be so easy. He'd been fantasizing about her for so many years that it would be difficult to stop. The Gabriela of his dreams was gentle and loving. The impression of the sweet seventeen-year-old still stayed with him, and he found that, for some reason, he had always wished their paths would cross again. Now that they had, and he was faced with reality, he wished Gabriela had stayed in his fantasy world.

Dedicated to my children:
Marshall and Kai, may you always run your own race and follow your dreams, no matter how difficult it might seem when you begin.

Acknowledgements

I am grateful that I've had the opportunity to write novels for the past twenty-five years. I thank God for the storytelling gift he has given me, and if it's not fully developed, it is strictly my fault.

I thank my family for standing by me for the many years that I've dedicated to the craft of writing and for supporting me through the highs and lows of publishing life.

I am grateful to Kensington Publishing for launching the Encanto line of romance books in the late 1990s. Their vision and anticipation of a market for Latino books, and their commitment to create a line of Latino romances written by Latino authors showed that they were ahead of the times. They have always been pioneers in ethnic romance fiction. Thank you for taking a chance on me, a new author at the time, and my novel Conquest.

About the author

Lara Rios writes romantic fiction and chick-lit romances that empower women to reach for all their goals, not only the love of their lives, but a life filled with possibilities.

Lara loves to travel, to be out in nature, and to dream up stories that include both. Life is an exciting adventure, and through her books, Lara takes her readers on thrilling, passionate journeys. Lara can be contacted at Lara-Rios.com